"What are ~~you doing~~ in here?' ~~she yelled~~

Lee had jumped back from the bathroom door the instant she'd spotted the room's occupant. Standing at the sink was the man she'd seen not a half hour earlier. The baseball hero of the Hammond High School grounds. The overgrown Little Leaguer.

"Well, well, if it isn't Leanna Elizabeth," he drawled. In exaggerated deference he hitched his low-slung towel a bit higher.

Lee tried not to stare at the bronzed chest or the long muscular legs, berry-brown even in mid-March. "What are you *doing* here?" she repeated.

"Obviously I just got out of the shower. Haven't you ever heard of knocking? Anyway, what are *you* doing, barging into my bathroom?"

"Your bathroom? Since when? This is my grandmother's house!"

He propped a hand on the sink and gave her an indignant look. "I happen to live here, too."

Kate Denton is a pseudonym for the writing team of Carolyn Hake and Jeanie Lambright. Both are Texans by adoption, Carolyn having come from Louisiana, Jeanie from Oklahoma. And both are employed full-time with federal government agencies. Each has three children and an assortment of cats and dogs. They're both history buffs and their hobbies include cooking and old movies (Carolyn) and traveling, ballet and writing country-western song lyrics (Jeanie). This is their third Romance and they're hard at work on the fourth!

Books by Kate Denton

HARLEQUIN ROMANCE
2870—WINNER TAKE ALL
2966—A BUSINESS ARRANGEMENT

Home
Safe

Kate Denton

Harlequin Books

TORONTO • NEW YORK • LONDON
AMSTERDAM • PARIS • SYDNEY • HAMBURG
STOCKHOLM • ATHENS • TOKYO • MILAN

ISBN 0-373-03057-6

Harlequin Romance first edition June 1990

CHAPTER ONE

WISPY FLAKES OF SNOW fluttered past the fortieth-floor window in seeming defiance of the fact that it was eight days into spring. From her corner office, Leanna Martin stared out at the gray, forbidding New York skyline. Despite the warmth of her office and the lavender wool suit she wore, Lee shivered. It wasn't the sight of snow or the fifteen-degree forecast that caused her tremor, but rather the sudden, sinking feeling of being so utterly alone.

Slowly, she walked across the room to her desk and picked up her coffee cup, then took a sip and grimaced. The coffee was cold. A tear trickled down her cheek, marking its course through her makeup. She put down the cup and reached for a tissue to stop the flow. Lee was just a breath away from breaking into uncontrollable sobbing.

She didn't even know why. It wasn't as if Delia Martin's death had been premature or that Lee and her grandmother had been particularly close. Still, the phone call a few minutes earlier had been a shock. Lee pondered her reaction; maybe it was simply because this was the final blow in a series of misfortunes. Her failed marriage, the deaths of her father, mother and stepfather...and now Grandmother. She'd thought she was immune to loss by now.

So why was she losing control like this? she wondered, dabbing at her eyes. Grandmother Martin had enjoyed a long life—almost eighty years. Could it be guilt? Yes, she felt guilty. There was no way around that. Lee knew she should have made a greater effort to visit. Or at least called more often. But until recently, she'd felt uncertain that the attention would have been well received. After all, contact goes both ways; Lee was the only grandchild, yet Grandmother had ignored her for most of her life. Lee had never understood why. It wasn't in keeping with her early memories of Delia as a kindly, loving woman, and of their special granddaughter-grandmother bond. Then suddenly, without warning, that had all ended. Lee had never quite managed to put the hurt behind her. At first, in the way children do, she felt she must have done something terrible, something that made Grandmother stop loving her. As she grew up, Lee came to understand that children frequently feel responsible for a divorce or estrangement, and she'd become resigned to the situation.

But the puzzlement had intensified in the past four years—since Lee attended her father's funeral and encountered Grandmother again—and the two had begun to reestablish a relationship. At first the letters and telephone calls had been infrequent and a bit stilted. But after Lee's mother and stepfather met their deaths in a fiery spectator accident at Le Mans the year before, Delia had been more insistent about becoming a part of Lee's life.

At her urging, Lee had arranged a trip to Delia's home in Hammond, Arkansas, for the Thanksgiving holiday, but she'd had to back out at the last minute when a team of bank examiners announced a forth-coming visit and all leave was canceled.

The trip to Arkansas had been rescheduled for the summer. Lee had penciled it in her calendar almost a month ago and made her plane reservations. Now she'd have to change the flight again—to this week.

Why hadn't she gone at Christmas instead of skiing in Vermont with Michael? Why had she put off the reunion until it was too late? Until Grandmother, her only living relative, had suffered a stroke and Lee was alone. Totally alone. For someone who'd of necessity been blasé about family, the knowledge that she now had none was surprisingly disturbing.

She balled up the damp tissue and threw it into the trash can. That was enough self-pity for one after-noon, she told herself, moving behind her desk. Aim-lessly she picked up the engraved nameplate, her pink-polished fingertips tracing the indented letters: *Leanna E. Martin, Vice President*. Vice President—two words that spelled achievement in the big city. She *was* suc-cessful, but somewhere in the back of her mind was the niggling little thought that success meant more than being well paid and respected by her colleagues. It also meant pursuing other interests, cultivating friends, taking time to relax and occasionally do something frivolous. Did she and her all-work-no-play life-style really meet those standards? She didn't think so.

"OF COURSE, if you want me to go with you, I'm sure I could arrange something." Michael Dayton sat across the table from her, holding her left hand and absently toying with the large diamond solitaire on her third finger as he talked.

"No, that's not necessary." She stared blankly down at her menu. Michael was not the kind of man who would willingly accompany his fiancée to a funeral. Even a grandparent's funeral. He wasn't the kind of person whose shoulder one cried on. Normally that suited Lee just fine; she didn't want to depend on a man, didn't want to need a man emotionally...to need anyone. Why did she feel differently today?

"When are the services?" He picked up a roll and buttered it.

Was he always this cold about death? Lee wondered. Sure, he was a physician—a neurosurgeon—so death wasn't exactly a stranger to him. But couldn't he be a tiny bit compassionate toward her family at least? Family—there was that word again. She'd dredged it up more in the past two hours than in the past ten years.

"Thursday. I'll fly to Little Rock Thursday morning and rent a car. Then I can drive straight on to Hammond. The funeral's at two-thirty."

"Didn't you tell me you're the only surviving relative?"

Lee nodded.

"Then you'll need to meet with her lawyer. Is there any property besides the house?"

"I doubt it, other than the furnishings. But why should I care about that?" Lee snapped, then immediately regretted her sharp tongue. Michael was Michael. Why did she suddenly want him to be somebody else?

"You're upset." He patted her hand again. "I really should go with you." He pulled out a pocket organizer and checked his Week at a Glance. "I suppose I could get Dan James to take over that presentation in Chicago."

"I said it wasn't necessary. I'm fine. It's just a bit unsettling to lose your last remaining relative, to see your family become extinct overnight."

"If you'd just set a wedding date, then we could start our *own* family," Michael prodded.

"I'm really not up to discussing that now, Michael," she hedged. "We'll talk about it when I return, okay?" Why did she keep putting him off? Why had she resisted his urging for the past year? Why had she been wondering lately whether she should marry Michael at all? There seemed to be lots of whys for her today, and she had no answers for any of them.

LEE TOSSED HER COAT into the back seat of the new Buick and eased out of the close-fitting suit jacket. She should have remembered what a difference in weather a thousand-odd miles could make. Little Rock was springlike today with a cloudless azure sky and the temperature in the mid-seventies. Lee adjusted the seat to accommodate her five-foot-five frame, then started the engine.

She pulled slowly out of the airport parking lot, still trying to decipher the highway directions she'd received from the rental-car clerk. The plane had arrived late and now she had only an hour and a half to get to Hammond and the funeral. She should have allowed herself more time.

As soon as she spotted the city-limits sign, she accelerated to sixty-five miles an hour and set the cruise control. Fortunately the highway traffic was light; she could breeze along and collect her thoughts. It was a bright day, the roadside foliage a combination of dark evergreen and the lighter new green of trees just starting to bud. Lee began to feel more composed as she leaned back in the bucket seat and watched the scenery race by.

What had Delia Martin really been like? Lee's images from the past were hazy: Delia in a faded floral wraparound apron rolling out pie crust, a smudge of flour on her plump pink cheek; Delia gardening, on her knees in the dirt, a trowel in her gloved hand; always smiling. Lee had felt that smile long-distance the last time they'd talked. Delia had been making dinner. "For Allen. He'll be off work before long."

"Oh, I'm beginning to think this Allen is someone I should meet." The name Allen had been mentioned during the past two phone calls.

"Honey, I'd love for you to meet him. I think you'd like him—and I know he'd like you." It was then they'd set the date for the summer visit.

Lee's eyes welled up. Delia had obviously considered this man someone special. Could she have been thinking about remarriage? Roy Senior had died when Lee was a baby. Did Grandmother have a suitor after all these years? Perhaps Lee would find out in Hammond. Not that it mattered anymore. She fished in her purse for a tissue to blot her moist eyes.

Finding the old, white-bricked church was no problem at all. It occupied a large corner lot facing the town square and succeeded in dwarfing the courthouse and the other buildings composing Hammond's business district. The church evoked a glimmer of memory, a fleeting recollection of childhood. It was an enduring fixture in both the religious and social life of Hammond. One Easter morning when Lee was five or six, Grandmother had brought her to services here. There'd been an egg hunt; that was all she remembered. But then, it had taken place some twenty-five years ago.

Lee parked the car next to the gray hearse in front of the church and entered the vestibule through the massive double doors. She glanced into the flower-filled sanctuary where soft organ music played as people filtered in and took their seats. She introduced herself to the funeral director, who led her to a front pew, where she sat alone.

It was a touching service. Reverend Barnes, the preacher, did a creditable job of paying tribute to her grandmother. Delia Martin had obviously gained the town's respect and affection. The sanctuary was filled with mourners, a large number of them elderly friends of her grandmother.

The quiet words should have been soothing. According to the eulogy, her grandmother was a woman at peace with the world and with herself, somebody worth knowing. Lee felt another twinge of guilt, coupled again with a measure of self-pity. She and Delia hadn't enjoyed a typical granddaughter-grandmother relationship, and she was still coping with the pent-up anger that had festered throughout her teen years, anger based on rejection. But she'd been hoping those feelings would fade as they got to know each other again. Now that chance would never come. Her eyes began to well up and the tears spilled over. Who was she really crying for? she wondered as she dabbed at her wet cheeks with a handkerchief.

Lee thought back to the events that had led to the estrangement from her grandmother. Her parents' divorce had been the catalyst. Roy and Marie Martin's marriage had always been turbulent, and the divorce was anything but amicable. Lee's parents had been separated when she was nine, and ever since their bitter breakup, she'd ceased to be part of her father's family—or of anyone's family. Although Marie was awarded custody, Lee had had little contact with either parent from that time on. Roy faded from her life, leaving Lee in her mother's care. Unfortunately for Lee, her mother grew tired of the single-parent experience and left her young daughter in the hands of others while she opted for a carefree, jet-set life-style with a wealthy second husband. And Delia, her only living grandparent, had . . . Lee wished she knew exactly what had happened with Grandmother. It was almost as though their earlier closeness had never existed.

After the ceremony, Lee stood beside Reverend Barnes outside the church shaking hands with the guests.

"Oh, Leanna, I remember you from your pictures," said one woman. "You still have that beautiful blond hair." The woman embraced her. "Your grandmother was so proud of you."

"You look just like your father," someone else told her.

"Yes, you're definitely Roy Martin's kid," his companion said. "Got those same eyes—almost a silver blue. All of us girls were crazy about those eyes when we were growing up. We thought they were every bit as sexy as Paul Newman's.''

And on it went. Lee felt strange, almost uncomfortable, knowing no one and yet being known by everyone. A somber man in a black suit came up to her. "Miss Martin. I'm Hubert Parker, your grandmother's lawyer.''

"Of course." Lee shook his hand. "Thank you for calling me in New York. I really appreciate your taking care of things until I could get down here.''

"No problem," he said. "Delia was very dear to me.''

"I assume there are some details we should discuss," Lee began.

"That's right," the lawyer answered. "We'll need to go over your grandmother's will...but I'm sure you'd like a few more days alone with your bereavement before we tackle these tedious legal matters.'' He patted her hand. "Anyway I happen to be on my way to Fort Smith for a conference and I'll be gone a day or two. Why don't I give you a call when I get back?''

Lee tried not to show her dismay. It was Thursday and she had hoped to clear up the details on Friday so she could be back at her job by Monday. That notion no longer seemed feasible. There was little point, however, in leaving Hammond and returning; it would be better to stay a bit longer and cover everything in this one trip. "Monday then? I'll be at Grandmother's house.''

"Sure. Monday should be fine." He reached into his pocket. "You'll probably want your own key." He handed her a lone brass key dangling from a ring advertising a local bank.

How else could I get in? Lee thought irritably, feeling a sudden sense of frustration. And *Monday* should *be fine*? She drew a deep breath as she tried to remind herself that not everyone was operating on her schedule. She would have to calm down and simply delay her departure. Another day or two wouldn't kill her. She seldom took time off from work, so there would be no problem with being away a little longer, especially since the trip involved a family funeral. She'd just call and have her leave extended.

"I'll wait to hear from you then, Mr. Parker," she said, trying to remain polite. "I really do need to get back to New York as soon as possible, though."

He nodded, giving her a studied look, then patted her hand again. "I'll call. In the meantime you just take it easy." He tipped his head in a slight bow and walked away.

An hour later, the burial services over, Lee found herself standing on Elm Street next to the rental car, staring up at the old two-story house that had belonged to her grandmother. It hadn't changed—a white house with a large front porch and black-framed windows. Two oversize hydrangea bushes ready to burst into bloom were positioned at each side of the porch and a couple of ancient pecan trees shaded the yard.

As Lee came around the car, she glanced across the street at a baseball game in progress on the school grounds. A group of teenage boys was playing a practice game, observed by several girls sitting on the wooden bleachers behind home plate. An adult was with them, a man dressed in dingy white baseball pants, socks and cleats, and a battered red-and-gray baseball cap. His shirt was unbuttoned, revealing a bare chest streaked with sweat. Lee noticed with consternation that the man had turned his attention away from the game to her. He moved from home plate around the edge of the ball diamond and circled the first-base dugout to the water fountain, then bent to take a long swallow, all the while keeping her in his line of vision. Now only the width of the street and a few grassy yards separated them.

When one of the boys came up to talk with him, Lee took the opportunity to study the man—his tanned, well-formed chest and the auburn hair decorating that chest, a shade darker than the hair showing beneath the edges of the baseball cap.

For some reason, she couldn't force her gaze away from him. It wasn't that he was handsome in the classic sense. His face was too square, and his eyebrows ran straight across his forehead like dashes instead of arches above the deep brown eyes. But those flaws only accentuated his six feet of rugged appeal. He was undoubtedly one of the most sensational male specimens Lee had ever seen, and she was disgusted with herself for even noticing. Men like this definitely weren't her style. She avoided them for the Michael type—slender and bookish-looking. This guy could be a *Playgirl* centerfold. And he was looking at her as though she were a companion photo in *Playboy*.

Despite her slimness, Lee was curvaceous. She had full breasts and well-rounded hips. And this guy was giving her a closer scrutiny than she'd get from a leering New York City construction worker. The way he seemed to be examining her was enough to make her wonder if he was trying to guess the color of her underwear. He made her want to dash into the house to escape his eyes. *Haven't you ever seen a woman before?* she felt like yelling. But instead, she somehow managed to break eye contact and move on around the car and up the walk. As she reached the porch, she stole a glance back across the street. The ball game had resumed; players were set in their positions on the red dirt field and her observer was crouched behind home plate coaching the kids. "Okay, Blake, straighten your arm. Cory, one foot on the base. Mouse, move back toward center field."

After several tries, Lee managed to fit the key into the front-door lock. She pushed open the door—and stared. It was as though she'd gone back a quarter of a century. The house still had the unique aroma she associated with those early-childhood visits, and with her father, and most of all with her grandmother. The smell was a mixture of age and lavender and mothballs.

She dropped her black leather purse onto a Victorian love seat in the foyer. Even though it was a bright afternoon, the entry remained dark and rather gloomy. Lee moved purposefully into the living room and opened the drapes. Sunlight flooding into the room revealed a fine dusty film on the mahogany tables. She pulled out a tissue from a packet in her pocket and swiped at the tables, then stopped. No use worrying about dust now, she thought, dropping the tissue into a flowered wastebasket.

Lee headed back through the house toward the kitchen. In her vague recollections, there was an old breakfront and a wooden table with cane-bottom chairs. Yes, there they were, and the kitchen was just as she remembered except for the addition of a portable television and a built-in dishwasher.

She opened the refrigerator. It was fully stocked— milk, juice, eggs, a half-full package of cookies. Lee had planned to spend the night at the house, but somehow it seemed a little morbid to eat her grandmother's food. Should she throw everything out? That would be ridiculous, she decided. She'd just run to the corner grocery and pick up something to nibble, then instruct Mr. Parker to have the refrigerator cleaned out and the contents donated to a needy family. The food shouldn't be wasted just because she was uncomfortable eating it.

Lee returned to the house an hour later carrying a paper sack of groceries in one arm. She opened the trunk of the rental car to retrieve her suitcase, then climbed the front-porch steps. Setting the overnighter on the porch and balancing the grocery bag on her hip, she managed to open the door and get inside. She walked to the kitchen, put the bag on the table and switched on the portable television on the counter.

The familiar voice of the network newscaster was comforting, reassuring her that she wasn't teetering at the outer fringes of civilization. She kicked off her shoes in a corner and headed upstairs. If she remembered correctly there were four bedrooms, one at each end of the hall and two in the middle. Grandmother's room had been on the far left, and her father's on the far right.

She walked down the hall, opened the door to Grandmother's bedroom and peered in. A large four-poster bed covered by a white chenille spread dominated the room. A patchwork quilt in an intricate circular pattern lay folded across the foot of the bed. She looked around for a few seconds, then quickly shut the door. She wasn't ready for this room yet. She opened another door. It was a small study with a sofa, desk and a second television. The room next to it turned out to be a guest room. She would stay there for the night.

Lee tossed her suitcase on the bed and flipped open the latches. She pulled out a bathrobe, then took off her suit jacket and started unbuttoning her blouse as she went down the hall to the bathroom.

She opened the bathroom door and jumped back as she spotted an occupant. "What are *you* doing in here?"

"Well, if it isn't Leanna Elizabeth," he said, his slow drawl making the words somehow sound like the name of a Cabbage Patch Doll. Standing at the sink was the baseball hero. In deference to her, he hitched the low-slung terry towel draped around his hips a little higher. "Obviously, I just got out of the shower. Haven't you ever heard of knocking? Anyway, what are *you* doing barging into my bathroom?"

"Your bathroom? Since when? This is my grandmother's house."

"True enough. But I happen to live here, too." He propped a hand on the sink and gave her an indignant glare.

Lee returned the look. She was trying hard to keep her eyes focused on his face and away from the now-familiar bronzed chest with its mat of damp hair, or the towel-covered midsection, or the long muscular legs, berry brown even in March. "Oh, that's very interesting."

"I'm glad you think so. Most people consider renting a rather ordinary subject."

"That's not what I meant." She ran her fingers through the waves of her permed hair. "I mean I'm just surprised to find out my grandmother took in boarders. And I'm afraid this complicates things, because I was planning on staying here myself."

He merely shrugged.

"How far to the nearest motel?" she snapped.

"Too far, unfortunately, so I suggest you come off your Puritan high horse. This is the twentieth century. And it's a pretty large house—room enough for two consenting adults." He paused. "Most New Yorkers wouldn't be uptight about sharing space."

"Then I guess I'm not like most New Yorkers."

"Well then, you're going to have to learn to knock before you enter a closed room. What would you have done if I hadn't been wearing this towel?"

"That would have been your embarrassment."

"No," he drawled for effect. "I wouldn't have been embarrassed." As his eyes met hers, the corners of his mouth turned up in what seemed to Lee a self-satisfied grin.

The infuriating man! Abrasive. Pushy. And smug! "Who are you, anyway?" she demanded.

"Allen Hilliard."

"Allen...?" Could this possibly be? This was her grandmother's Allen? Lee was astounded, but had no intention of revealing her surprise. "And who is *Allen Hilliard* other than someone my elderly grandmother obviously took in?"

"Why don't you let me get dressed and then we'll continue playing twenty questions. Unless, of course, you'd like to watch me put my clothes on." He reached to release the towel and gave her that irritating grin again.

Lee took a giant step backward. "I can't think of anything less interesting. I'll see you downstairs when you're presentable." She paused. "You do appear fully clothed every now and then, don't you?"

"Only under duress," he said. "But just for you, I'll make an exception."

"Thank you," she said, slamming the door.

Lee stood motionless in the hall and attempted to compose herself. Talk about surprises. And, darn it, more complications. She could use a cup of coffee about now. Maybe that would help her relax and collect her thoughts. She entered her room to fetch the latest *Ms.* magazine from her suitcase, then walked downstairs to the kitchen. She quickly located an aqua coffee canister, one of a set, in a cabinet and an old aluminum coffeepot resting on an unlit stove burner. Lee wasn't sure she really knew how to make coffee in such a contraption, but it couldn't be too difficult—no moving parts.

She put a pan of water on to boil and leafed through the magazine while she waited. But her thoughts kept straying from the articles to the man upstairs. Allen Hilliard's presence here certainly threw a monkey wrench into her plans. She had intended to close down the house immediately, or as soon as she could pack and remove the contents. However, if this guest had some kind of lease, there might be other considerations. She would have to ask Mr. Parker for advice.

Her own preference was to tell the unwelcome boarder to clear out. But she figured she had no legal right to do that. Besides, he didn't appear to be the kind of man one could just order around.

Speak of the devil—and in he walked, just in time to catch her spooning grounds into the top of the coffee pot. "Here," he said, "let me do that."

Don't wait for an invitation, she wanted to say. *Just help yourself to whatever you want.* But she didn't want to throw out that kind of dare. He might take her up on it—and then some.

Allen came over and took the measuring spoon from her. "The grounds go in the middle, not the top." He took the pot apart, dumped the grounds from the top into the middle section, reassembled the pot, then poured the water through. "Haven't you ever used a drip pot before?"

"I'm sorry to admit that all my experience has been with electric coffee makers."

He laughed. "Then you probably don't know what good coffee tastes like." He walked to the breakfront for cups and saucers and poured each of them a cup. "Try some of this. Cream? Sugar?" Obviously he was very much at home in her grandmother's kitchen because his hand went right to the cabinet containing the sugar bowl.

"Black is fine." She accepted the cup and saucer, then sat down at the kitchen table.

He leaned against the counter to drink his coffee. His only concession to clothing was a pair of faded cutoffs and a shirt, open as before.

"Don't you ever cover your chest like ordinary people?"

"Does it bother you, Leanna Elizabeth?" He was smiling and his dark eyes twinkled.

"Not in the least," she lied. Actually it did. She was growing increasingly uncomfortable, with parts of the Hilliard anatomy constantly in view. "And stop calling me that. Try Lee or Leanna, Mr. Hilliard."

"Okay, and you call me Allen. After all, we *are* housemates."

Lee frowned. "Which probably isn't such a good idea."

"Don't you trust yourself?"

The look she gave him clearly conveyed whom she didn't trust.

He picked up the *Ms.* magazine next to him on the counter. "*Ms....*" He tilted his head to study her. "Yes, you'd be a Ms. But I understand you were once a Mrs., weren't you, Leanna Elizabeth?"

"Stop calling me—"

"I forgot. I won't do it again. Don't you like your name?"

"I like it fine. It's the name my parents gave me. So I'd be saddled with it whether I liked it or not."

"Your parents didn't name you," Allen said. "Delia did."

"How do you know that?"

"Oh, I just do. Your parents couldn't agree on a name so Delia stepped in. Elizabeth was her middle name and Leanna was your other grandmother's name."

Lee knew enough about her family to realize he was probably telling the truth. Still, it annoyed her that this overgrown Little Leaguer knew so much about her, especially things she didn't know herself.

He got to his feet and poured more coffee, refilling her cup in the process. "You never answered the part about being a Mrs."

"I can't see how that could interest you."

"That you were once Carl Adams's wife? He's had quite an amazing football career."

"There's more to life than sports."

"And more to being a husband than tossing touch-down passes?"

"I really don't think that's any of your business, do you?" The phone rang and as Allen answered it Lee let out a sigh of relief. She had no intention of discussing her marriage. She'd been so young and it had lasted such a short time—and she'd felt so betrayed. Lee didn't want to talk about that part of her life.

Her mind floated back to another time. The summer before her junior year at Syracuse, the summer she met Carl Adams. She was leaving the bleachers after watching a football scrimmage when, inexplicably, he'd singled her out. Carl was a senior and the team's star quarterback, headed for a career in the pros. A jock's jock. He was also the premier ladies' man on campus. Within weeks Lee was madly in love. So in love that she failed to notice Carl's attentions to every other female for miles around. Lee was like a thirsty wanderer who'd stumbled onto an oasis, drinking in Carl as though he were life-giving water. A balm to her lonely existence.

When she'd discovered she was pregnant with Carl's child, he'd reluctantly agreed to marry her. But Carl made no secret of his disdain for one so foolish as to "get herself pregnant." She'd miscarried in the third month and her husband was openly relieved that he wouldn't be bothered with a child. He'd soon made it clear he didn't intend to be bothered with Lee, either. Carl's coveted pro contract had materialized, and it included a fat signing bonus. He'd become even more attractive to other women and pursued them blatantly. The divorce followed a few months later.

Lee was devastated, all her fantasies about love shattered. Wanting to be loved only guaranteed rejection, she decided. It had happened in her family and now with Carl. She'd determined then and there never to suffer such anguish again. A damper had been tightly closed on her feelings. Instead of concentrating her energies on relationships, she now devoted her time to a career. She'd become immune to real emotion. Since her divorce, love hadn't been a word in her vocabulary—not even with Michael Dayton, the man she'd agreed to marry.

Allen hung up the phone and turned to Lee. "Sorry about that interruption. Now, where were we?"

"I didn't see you at the funeral," she said, ignoring the question.

"Delia and I shared the same sentiments about funerals. Weddings, too. We thought the only people who needed to be there were the participants. Besides, I was working."

"Working?"

"I coach at the high school. Baseball."

"The Mudville Eleven?"

"Nine. Football's eleven—or don't you remember? And do I detect a slightly condescending attitude toward the Hammond Hornets?"

"No, not at all. I'll bet the Hornets are one of the most exciting things about Hammond."

"As a matter of fact, you're right. The team won District last year and we intend to go all the way to State this spring."

"Wow. State. Imagine that."

"Your sarcasm is showing, *Ms*. Martin. I'm sorry to be boring the big-city visitor with my humble accomplishments."

"Now who's being sarcastic?"

"Maybe we should start over," he said, walking toward her and extending a hand. "I'm Allen Hilliard. Welcome to Hammond, Ms. Leanna Elizabeth Martin. I'm sorry it had to be under such sad circumstances."

Lee's face fell as his comments took hold. "Me, too. Poor Grandmother." She gazed down at her coffee cup, then looked back up. "Mr. Parker said she had a stroke."

"That's right."

"Do you know any of the details? Mr. Parker ran off before I could question him."

"She went peacefully in her sleep... Do we really have to talk about it? Anyway, what difference does it make now? Delia's gone."

"You'd want to know if she were your grandmother."

"No, I wouldn't. Death is death and very final. The why of it we don't understand, and the how of it's really irrelevant in the long run." He placed his cup in the sink and quietly left the room.

CHAPTER TWO

LEE ROSE FROM THE TABLE and walked to the kitchen sink where she rinsed out her cup. That was strange, she thought. Allen's attitude was certainly cold. Especially for someone who'd been living in Grandmother's home. Grandmother had obviously been fond of him; had the affection not gone both ways?

Lee spent the next hour walking through the house. When she had returned for her father's funeral, she had been here only long enough for the services and for a harried visit with Grandmother. Because of business pressures, Lee had flown back to New York the same day. No time to see things and remember. Pictures, mementos... Although she'd been away for years, some of these keepsakes and furnishings were ingrained in her memory. The thick oak table in the dining room, for example. Lee remembered a rainy Sunday afternoon, sitting under it with her doll, playing house. At the time the old table had seemed immense. Now it looked like a basic round dining table, no bigger and no smaller than a thousand others. Funny how the memory increased objects in size as one grew up.

She remembered many of the figurines Delia had collected, some of them valuable, like the Lladro ballerina or the Steuben animals, others worth only token amounts. Lee studied them in the glass case in the living room. To Lee the child, these bric-a-brac were treasures to behold, especially the replica of the Statue of Liberty from the New York World's Fair and the tiny Kewpie doll from Atlantic City. Lee smiled as she opened the case and fingered a ceramic cardinal. She had given the bird to her grandmother on one of her trips here, a spur-of-the-moment birthday present her father had allowed her to select at Murial's Gift Shop on the square.

Her father. Two remembrances of him were part of the collection. A bronzed pair of his baby shoes and an old pocket watch he'd inherited from his father and grandfather. The watch didn't keep dependable time but he'd carried it anyway, for sentimental reasons. Lee set the watch to the correct time and put it back in the case. She then straightened a lace doily on one of the end tables before she walked back into the kitchen and stood by the window, looking outside.

The backyard was filled with trees, displaying a profusion of colors. Elms, oaks and sweet gums in half a dozen shades of green. The purplish pink of a redbud. White blossoms on an ancient pear tree. To a young girl running tag or playing hide-and-seek, the yard had resembled an endless forest. As Lee stared out the window, she was amazed how time had shrunk it to lot size. She'd missed so much. Anger surfaced but Lee determinedly brushed it away. She sighed and shook her head. So much had changed and, at the same time, remained the same.

"YOU'RE NOT ACTUALLY going to eat one of those things?"

Startled, Lee turned from the oven. She frowned at the frozen TV dinner in her hand, then at Allen. "And what if I am? I happen to be hungry."

"Well, for gosh sakes, eat something that resembles food, then." Allen took the dinner away from her, then opened the side-by-side refrigerator-freezer and peered in. "Here," he said, and pulled out a covered plastic bowl. "Pot roast." He removed the lid to give her a quick peek at a roast surrounded by potatoes, carrots and onions, then popped the bowl into the microwave and set the timer.

"You could have fooled me," Lee said. "I'd have bet you couldn't cook."

"I don't. Rose Adair, the home-ec teacher, and I have an understanding."

"Oh?" Lee raised an eyebrow.

"Nothing like that." His eyebrow raised in response. "Rose had this notion I needed looking after now, and she brought over some meals. I accepted, with the stipulation that I repair her roof this summer. Trade-offs are one of the benefits of small-town living." He grinned at her. "Relieved I'm not involved in a torrid intra-school relationship?"

She glared at him. "You have an inflated opinion of yourself. Why should I possibly care about your mundane love life?"

Allen winked. "Don't bet the rent money on mundane." He opened the breakfront and pulled out two plates. "Now make yourself useful and set the table." He thrust the dishes into her hands.

Obediently Lee began setting the dining-room table as Allen handed her cutlery and place mats and paper napkins. In a matter of fifteen minutes the meal was heated and they had taken their seats. "Hold on a second," he said. "We'll have some wine." He got up and walked to the kitchen, then returned with a bottle of chilled white wine and two stemmed glasses.

Lee glanced at the label. There were no familiar French names on the bottle. It was an Arkansas brand, one she'd never heard of. "Is this what they call Cuvée Bubba?"

Allen laughed. "Why don't you take a sip before you look down your nose at the label." Using a corkscrew, he pulled out the cork with a soft pop, then poured two glassfuls.

Lee had to admit the wine wasn't half bad, and she also began to realize this man wasn't quite what he appeared. Here he was, demonstrating a degree of sophistication and savoir faire—a small degree to be sure, especially when compared to the urbane Michael, but nonetheless, a smidge of class. To Lee, who ranked class alongside brains and business acumen as highly desirable traits in a man, this was an amazing discovery. But it still didn't change her opinion of Allen Hilliard. He was a jock—and athletic types had no place on Lee's list of favorite people.

The two made small talk as the meal progressed. Rose Adair was a terrific cook and the pot roast tasted ten times better than the dried-out turkey dinner Lee would have eaten had Allen not intervened. He assumed the role of host, prompting her into a second helping and making sure her wine glass stayed filled. After a while, Lee lost count of the number of glasses she'd drunk. It couldn't be many, she rationalized, if they were still on the same bottle... That was the same bottle wasn't it?

After dinner, they took their coffee and moved into the living room where the light was better for looking at photos. Sitting beside her—but not *too* close beside her—on the brocade couch, Allen showed her several recent pictures he'd taken of Delia.

"This was her birthday," he said, handing Lee a snapshot. "I made her get dolled up so I could take her out to dinner."

Lee gazed at the picture. Delia facing the camera, a stiff smile on her face, standing proudly beside a floral arrangement. She recognized the dress, the same one Delia had been buried in, and the arrangement, the one she'd ordered from the teleflorist.

"I thought she'd never get rid of those damn flowers. Kept 'em till they'd completely shriveled up and lost their identities."

Lee looked at him and at the picture, then began to cry. Tears flowed from her eyes and streamed down her cheeks.

Allen stared at her. "I'm sorry. What did I say?"

"Nothing," she sniffed. "It's just sinking in that Grandmother is really gone." She wept even more and the tears flowed unhindered down her cheeks.

"Come on now," he said. "Delia wouldn't have wanted you to carry on like this." He gave her a quick pat on the shoulder.

"I can't help it," Lee wailed. "I didn't even get a chance to tell her goodbye." She began to sob loudly.

Allen rose from the couch and stood awkwardly in front of her. "Please don't cry. I can't stand to see a woman cry."

Lee paused for a second to glance at him, then continued sobbing.

"I know what you need—a breath of fresh air. That'll make you feel better. Let's go outside." He gently lifted her by the shoulders to a standing position. But instead of moving, Lee leaned her head against his chest, tears dampening his shirt.

Allen stroked her hair, then wrapped his arms around her, rocking her softly as the crying lessened. "Here." He handed her a handkerchief from his pocket and she wiped her nose as he settled his arms around her shoulders again.

Lee looked up at him, her eyes red-rimmed and glazed, and he looked back tenderly, the two of them maintaining a locked gaze for a few seconds. Suddenly his eyes closed and he bent his head to claim her moist lips with his own in a tentative kiss. Without shock or hesitation, Lee returned the kiss. Her arms reached around his neck and she pressed against him in an unplanned reaction to the pleasure of his mouth on hers, his body close to hers. It felt so right, so natural, being held in his embrace....

Finally the kiss ended and Allen led her back to the couch. She sat next to him and allowed him to slip one arm around her shoulders. But when he tried to kiss her again, she placed her fingers on his lips. "Please, no." She leaned her head against his shoulders.

"Oooh." Lee lifted her head an inch off the pillow only to drop immediately back onto the downy softness. She lay there a moment, trying to focus her burning eyes. Her temples were throbbing. Her mouth felt as if it had been carpeted during the night. This was a bona fide hangover.

It was the wine she had consumed at dinner. Not that it was bad. Lee knew she couldn't blame her present condition on rural rotgut; the truth was that the native vintage Allen had served tasted first-rate. She'd simply had too much of it, especially in her vulnerable emotional state. And she wasn't accustomed to more than a glass or two at most—but excuses didn't improve the way she felt. Terrible.

The hangover was one thing, but something else was weighing even more heavily on Lee's mind. Exactly what had happened last night? Lee could remember her maudlin reminiscences about her grandmother. She remembered Allen comforting her. Then he'd kissed her. Not a kiss of conquest, but a caring kiss, a nice kiss.... Nice?

In the clear light of morning, even through the fog of a hangover, her suspicions were aroused. Nice kiss or no, she didn't trust Allen Hilliard any farther than she could throw him. Yet she had kissed him back. What had come over her? It must have been the long day, the trip, the funeral. She'd been feeling tired, sad, woozy and all that had combined to render her susceptible to the attentions of a near stranger.

She stared at the ceiling, deep in thought. What was Allen Hilliard doing in her grandmother's house? He claimed he was renting, yet acted as though he owned the place. Who exactly *was* he? A long-lost relative? A con man cozying up to an old lady? An underpaid teacher looking for a way to improve his position in life?

There was definitely more to him than met the eye. He was not a mere boarder, of that she was certain.

And as far as she knew, not a relative. But Delia had made it clear she felt close to him.

Lee tried to think back. There was something about him that seemed almost familiar, yet she was positive she'd never met him before. He wasn't the kind of man women generally forgot, not with all that animal magnetism deliberately unchecked.

How many times had she and Grandmother talked during the past year? Maybe once a month. And there had been Delia's occasional letters. The complete content of their phone conversations and the letters escaped her, but one thing was definite: Grandmother had never indicated Allen lived there. Or revealed he was a handsome hunk of a man in the prime of life.

Aside from the surprise of finding him in the house, Lee had experienced something else—a reaction to the way Allen looked at her. A wanting look. That was the best way to define it. But also a look that implied he knew exactly what she was thinking. If true, that could prove embarrassing. For despite her suspicions, despite her long-term dislike of his type of man—the sweaty, swaggering athletic type—there was something about him that spoke to what she considered her baser instincts.

Dear Lord, she thought, feeling guilty. What about Michael? My mind needs to be on the man I'm engaged to, not concentrating on the likes of an Allen Hilliard. Why am I letting him appeal to me? She raised her head again, this time managing to bring her body into a sitting position. *At least I woke up in bed alone,* she consoled herself. But she didn't allow herself to speculate on what *might* have happened.

Allen was nowhere around when Lee went downstairs. She guessed he had left for school. It was Friday, so classes must be in session. She pulled back the curtain in the living room and saw yellow buses parked along the street. She could hear the faint noise of young people talking and laughing, probably going from one class to the next.

Lee ate a quick breakfast of coffee and toast, then drove down to the grocery to pick up some cardboard boxes. If she was going to be stuck here for a day or so, she might as well start packing away her grandmother's things.

"Leanna, good morning." A balding man wearing a white apron tied around his ample girth and a cap reading Arkansas Razorbacks greeted her. He stuck out his hand. "You probably don't remember me. George Wilson? I was at your grandmother's funeral."

"Good morning, Mr. Wilson. It's good to see you again."

"Nice to see you out and about. What can I do for you?"

Lee was surprised at the friendliness she'd encountered all over town. Earlier at the service station when she'd filled her car, now here at the grocery store. She'd always felt secure in the anonymity of metropolitan life. Now she welcomed the words of sympathy, of comfort, of caring. "I thought perhaps I could talk you out of some boxes, so I can pack a few things of my grandmother's."

"Yes, dear." He nodded solemnly. "One of the sad tasks we have to face. I don't suppose you'll be able to take much back with you?"

He posed it as a question. Lee didn't really know how to respond. She didn't even know what exactly was in the old house, much less what she was going to do about it. "No, not a lot," she mumbled in reply.

The grocer continued chatting, first discussing the weather—unseasonably warm, even for Arkansas in the spring—then relating a story about Lee's father, followed by one about her grandmother. Between nods, a question was forming in Lee's mind.

"How long has Mr. Hilliard been here?"

"Allen? Let's see." George scratched his head in thought. "Little over two years, I think. Yeah, that's right. He showed up in January two years ago. In right bad shape, too." He walked into the back room and returned with several empty boxes. "These look about right. Don't want boxes too big. Wouldn't be able to lift them when they're filled."

"In bad shape, you say," Lee probed, trying to get the conversation back to Allen. "Where did he come from?"

"According to Allen, straight from hell...." He blushed. "Sorry, ma'am. But that's what Allen said. He used to live here, you know."

Just as Lee was planning another question, the screen door of the store opened and two elderly women entered. She recognized them from her grandmother's funeral, and they paused to chat with her, both inquiring about Allen. "He was such a comfort to Delia," one told her.

"Allen's a dear, sweet boy," the other said, then laughed. "And to think, no one believed that young rascal would ever be a decent adult."

When the ladies finally moved on to their shopping, Lee tried to get in another word with the grocer, but he was busy with other customers. Now she really was intrigued. . . .

"HUNGRY?" ALLEN WAS STANDING at the kitchen counter, layering slices of cold roast beef, tomatoes and lettuce onto pieces of whole-wheat bread.

"Hmmm," Lee responded, her appetite whetted.

He sliced the sandwich in two and slid it onto a blue-and-white-flowered plate. "Here, want to open these?" He pushed a bag of potato chips toward her.

"I thought you were at school."

"I come home every day for lunch."

Home. Clearly he considered this his home. "How long have you been living here?"

"With your grandmother?" He took a bite of his sandwich. A couple of moments passed. "About a year and a half."

"I understand you were in Hammond before that."

"Checking up on me?" He smiled.

Darn, she hadn't meant to be so obvious. But then, she didn't have much experience in cloak-and-dagger stuff. "Maybe," she replied. "Grandmother didn't tell me much about you. Naturally I'm curious."

"Curious or nosy? As for your grandmother not giving you a rundown on me, when did she have a chance?"

"During our phone conversations, of course."

"Are you referring to those three-minute calls on all the official holidays?"

"What do you mean by that?"

"Just what I said. You called Delia like clock-work—or should I say calendar work—on Valentine's Day, Mother's Day, her birthday, Thanksgiving and Christmas. Oh, there were nice little cards, too. And once in a while, on the proper occasions, naturally, a present or flowers. But never time out of your busy schedule to visit, to spend a few of your valuable hours with your grandmother."

"That's not true." Lee's blue eyes hardened into an icy stare. "I had a trip planned this summer—" She stopped. "Anyway, who are you to be lecturing me about my relationship with Grandmother? I don't remember your being adopted into the family."

"Sorry, I guess I forgot my place. I suppose I thought my friendship with Delia gave me the right to say something."

"Some friend. You're a fine one to criticize. You even found excuses to avoid her funeral!"

"I was around when she was alive. Delia knew I loved her. I didn't have to make some stupid show of crying over her casket."

Lee didn't know what to say. Was that how he viewed her visit here—an act? Pretending to be the bereaved granddaughter when she really didn't care? It wasn't like that at all. Still, some of the things he said hit home. Lee could have done more. But then, so could Grandmother. Allen didn't understand how it felt to have a grandmother drop out of your life one day and twenty-odd years later decide to drop back in. He wouldn't know how hard it was to make up for years of no communication, to establish immediate intimacy. Grandmother probably catered to his every need, probably nurtured him constantly, gave him lots of warmth and support. But all this had been denied Lee. She couldn't help feeling a twinge of envy.

Suddenly his words burst into her mind. "You *loved* her?" she said. Until she met him, Lee had guessed Allen to be Grandmother's beau, but after the introductions, she'd ruled out romance. Surely not! He was what...thirty, maybe? Certainly no older than thirty-two or -three. A fifty-year age gap didn't make for a romance, not even in New York and assuredly not in Hammond.

"Clean up your dirty little mind. I loved her, yes. I cared about her, yes. But as a friend. And she cared about me. Delia was probably the dearest person in the whole world to me. She took me in when I didn't care whether I lived or died. I miss her more than you can possibly imagine. She taught me how to love—not only how to love others, but probably more important, how to love myself. Do you love yourself, Lee? Is there time in your big-city life for *any* kind of love?"

Lee opened her mouth to respond but no words came out.

"Think about it," he said, and without waiting for an answer he set his empty plate on the counter and walked purposefully out of the room. Through the glass panes, Lee's eyes followed him out the door and watched him lope across the school yard. Did she love herself? He seemed to know the answer: no, not particularly. She'd never had any reason to believe she was very lovable. Her life might have been very different if Grandmother had been around to teach her about love, too.

Lee spent the afternoon in her grandmother's bedroom sorting her effects. One dresser drawer was filled
with starched and pressed handkerchiefs, another with
crocheted scarves and doilies, and yet another with
exquisite bed linens—embroidered pillow cases and
sheets. A cedar chest was packed with two patchwork
quilts, and a box in the closet was brimming with
family pictures.

She picked up a couple of the loose snapshots and
glanced at them. One was of her father as a young boy,
wearing a cowboy hat and perched on a pony. He'd
been six years old according to the notation on the
back. The other was a later picture from high school.
She studied it, trying to determine if, indeed, she had
her father's eyes. Yes, those eyes looking back from
the picture did seem to have the same azure intensity
as her own. She also saw herself in the way the lips
curved and realized the slight cleft in her chin was
definitely a Martin trait. Lee had always hated the cleft
until she saw an old Ava Gardner movie and realized
the facial feature was rather attractive.

Lee returned the photos to the stack. There was no
time for woolgathering right now, for losing herself in
memories and regrets. She dumped the loose pictures
and albums into a larger box, then headed toward another linen drawer.

The front door slammed, then the tramp of foot-
steps sounded on the stairs. Lee waited apprehen-
sively, wondering if Allen would come looking for her.
He owed her an apology for his loutish behavior at
lunch. Would he offer one?

Apparently not. She heard drawers opening and
closing from his bedroom, then the sound of the

bathroom door shutting and water running in the shower.

Lee returned to her task of filling and marking a box. She stood up, her body stiff in protest at the hours spent sitting on the floor, and glanced at her watch. Five-thirty. Hard to believe she'd been in the bedroom all afternoon. Might as well go down to the kitchen for a cup of tea. She felt a little hungry, too. Maybe a cookie to go with the tea. Surely Allen wouldn't begrudge her one of his chocolate-covered graham crackers from the refrigerator.

She finished an article in *Ms.* as she drank her tea and nibbled on the cookie. It was half an hour before Allen finally came down the stairs. He appeared in the kitchen and gave her a quick, unsmiling nod. Lee couldn't help noticing how attractive he was, his hair a wet mat of curls and his taut, muscular frame accentuated by the green polo shirt and tapered slacks. The awareness annoyed her.

"I'm going out," he said. "Do you need anything before I leave?"

She shook her head. "But I did eat one of your cookies."

"Help yourself—and to anything else you might want for supper." He turned and disappeared out the back door.

"Well," Lee said to the empty room, "looks like Mr. Hilliard has himself a date." She sat quietly for a few seconds, listening to the sound of the garage door opening, then rose to watch a white Corvette back out of the drive. The car surprised Lee; she'd expected something more befitting a small-town coach—a pickup truck or maybe a Jeep. Certainly not something this costly. Allen's car might not be the latest model, but Corvettes were expensive, especially on a school-teacher's salary.

Despite her reservations about his character, Lee was sorry her housemate had left for the evening. She looked around the large kitchen, suddenly feeling the loneliness of the place with Allen gone. *Cool it,* she scolded herself. *The less you see of this man, the better off you'll be. You don't want to complicate your life with unpleasant relationships.*

Lee watched the evening news, then ate a bowl of soup while viewing a situation comedy. Bored with television, she took a long, leisurely bath, put on pajamas and robe, then got in bed to pore over some loan applications she'd brought along in her briefcase. Somehow it was difficult to focus on them, probably because the soft chirping of the crickets outside interrupted her concentration. There were no harsh city sounds—no traffic, no sirens. Although soothing, the quiet was almost distracting in its unfamiliarity. Michael would hate it here.

Michael! How could she have forgotten her promise to call him today? She put the papers back into the briefcase, then went downstairs to use the kitchen phone. Michael's number rang three times before his answering machine came on. Apparently she was too late; he'd already left for the medical meeting. Lee recited a brief message, telling him what time she'd called and giving the phone number here. Then she padded back upstairs. Might as well go to bed, she thought. She was bored with reading and too tired to do any more packing tonight.

But sleep was elusive. Where had Allen gone? She wondered what one did on dates down here. A wiener roast? A hayride? That probably happened only in the movies, she thought. But it wasn't easy to imagine a night life without theaters, without galleries, without real restaurants. The only eating establishments she'd seen were a hamburger joint and a fried-chicken franchise. So where had he gone?

Finally Lee dozed off. But her sleep was interrupted when she heard Allen roar in, the tires of his sports car crunching on the gravel drive. She looked at the clock. Three-fifteen. Whatever he'd found to do, it must have been fun. Her irritation began to revive as she imagined him at some local honky-tonk, wowing the girls with talk of the fighting Hornets and the State Championship, then finally persuading some hapless female to let him take her home.

What a disquieting notion. What kind of woman would fall for his arrogant macho ways, anyway? Even as she asked the question, Lee decided on an answer. Someone who hadn't been exposed to the likes of Dr. Michael Dayton, a suave, self-possessed gentleman who didn't wear his sexuality on his sleeve. Probably an inexperienced woman, someone young and naive, who didn't understand there was more to a man than a well-developed physique. *Forget it, Lee Martin,* she mused. That's a minority opinion. Ninety-nine percent of the women she knew would do flip-flops over Allen Hilliard. And that was probably a conservative estimate.

Lee turned on the bedside light and reached for an old copy of *Reader's Digest* lying on the nightstand. Might as well read, she decided, until sleep returned.

Which it did, about an hour later. When she awoke, the sun was in full burst and a bright spring day jolted her senses.

She was in the kitchen sipping a cup of black coffee when Allen appeared, barefooted, bare-chested as usual, wearing only gray sweatpants. His hair was tousled and his face sprouted a heavy shadow of beard. Yet, scruffy as he was, his rough-hewn sensuousness still beckoned, and Lee once more hated herself for being so susceptible to it. Why did this man evoke these tantalizing thoughts in her, she wondered, again feeling a twinge of guilt about Michael. Why did Allen's presence stir up such primitive urges? Surely her brain was getting mushy. Probably from too much fresh air.

He stretched and groaned, then shuffled sleepy-eyed over to the coffeepot.

"Rough night?" she asked lightly.

"Not really."

"Well, you sure were out late." She took another sip of her coffee.

Allen poured his coffee into an oversize white stoneware mug, then turned to face her. "Were you waiting up for me?"

"Hardly," she said. "I just happened to hear you drive in at three o'clock."

He smiled slyly. "Oh."

She was beginning to despise that smile. "What's so amusing at eight-thirty in the morning?"

"You. You sound like a jealous wife. You're sure not like your grandmother. Delia never cared when I came in."

"Well, neither do I."

He walked over to the table and sat down across from her. "I know what's wrong. You're feeling neglected. You're upset that I went out and left you here all by yourself. Were you worried I was with someone else?"

Her brows knitted. "You really are something, do you know that?"

Allen stroked her arm. "Don't worry. I won't tell anyone you're upset, and I'll make it up to you tonight. Tonight *you'll* come with me."

Lee pulled her arm away. "Please, don't do me any favors. Just find another one of your local females to carouse with and I'll take care of myself. Besides, I'm much too busy to go anywhere." She got up from the table and carried her cup and saucer to the sink.

"We'll see," he mumbled as she turned to go.

LEE WAS IN THE DINING ROOM, sorting through bric-a-brac when Allen entered. "Time for a break. You've been at this all day."

She shook her head in frustration. "I know. There's so much here."

Allen laughed. "Delia wasn't much of one to throw anything away. You wouldn't believe what we had to clear out of my room before I could move in. I think everything your dad ever owned was in there." He paused. "So why don't you call it a day and join me for a drink?"

"No, thanks. I think I had enough the other night."

"Don't worry about that," he teased. "You make a sweet drunk."

Lee's eyes flashed in anger. It was one thing for her to admit overindulgence the evening before last, but something else entirely for Allen to accuse her of being drunk. "I wasn't drunk."

"Of course not. Sorry. Tell you what. If you're not in the mood for a drink, why don't you take a minute to freshen up and we'll go get a bite to eat."

"It's not even six o'clock."

"This isn't New York. We tend to dine a little earlier in these parts."

"You go on then. I'll make myself something later."

Allen scowled. "Do you think you could possibly relax for a few minutes and pretend to be a regular person instead of Ms. High and Mighty Big City Banker?" Before she had a chance to respond, he continued, "All I'm suggesting is a trip to the Catfish Cabin over on the river. I enjoy a little company when I'm eating—preferably pleasant company, but beggars can't be choosers."

"Does that mean you're begging me to go with you?"

He chuckled. "If you ever catch me begging, Lee, it'll be for something much more important than dinner."

"Well, begging or no, dinner's still the most you'll get. From me, anyway."

"Does that mean you've decided to come?"

Lee thought for a moment. "Why not?" she agreed. "It's time I saw how the other half lives."

"Yeah," he agreed, "find out what you've been missing." Then he laughed again.

Did anything ever get to him? Lee wondered. Probably not, she quickly decided. "Give me about half an hour," she said. "Enough time to shower first."

He gave her a perusal. "You do look a little the worse for wear. I'd better wash up, too. Maybe after we eat we can run over to Arkadelphia. There's a traveling carnival in town—I'll take you for a ride on the ferris wheel."

Lee slapped her hands against her sweatpants, causing a cloud of dust. "Thanks, but no thanks. I don't have time for carnivals. I've got to finish organizing all this." She gestured around the room.

"It'll wait."

"I won't let it." She was adamant. Dinner she'd agreed to—she did have to eat—but that was all the time she planned to spend with him.

"That's too bad. You don't have much fun, do you, lady?" He turned and disappeared down the hallway.

No, dammit, I don't have much fun. Not the kind he was talking about. Her busy life left no time for spontaneity. But what business was it of Allen's? Angrily, she ordered herself to stop thinking about him, stop letting him irritate her so. She should be thinking of her fiancé, not of Allen Hilliard. She imagined sitting next to Allen on the ferris wheel, then guiltily tried to put Michael into the picture instead. It didn't work.

Later, in the shower, Allen still occupied her mind. She couldn't erase an image of water cascading down his tanned, firm body. Couldn't help imagining him there with her. Was there no end to her craziness? *This insanity shall pass,* she told herself. And very quickly, she hoped.

"DON'T YOU THINK you're a bit overdressed?" Allen was leaning against the banister, watching her descend the staircase. She'd put on the skirt to her suit and a print blouse, the only clothes she had with her that were anywhere near suitable for going out.

"I'm afraid this is it. I only brought my suit and a couple of pairs of sweats."

"Then change to the sweats. You'll be more comfortable."

Lee looked at him disbelievingly.

"Trust me," Allen insisted.

Shrugging, she turned back up the stairway to change.

He called after her, "We'll have to run over to Wal-Mart tomorrow and get you a pair of jeans."

Trust me, Lee thought with wry amusement. She might be willing to change her clothes on his say-so. But to trust Allen Hilliard? Not on a bet.

CHAPTER THREE

ALLEN TURNED onto Main Street on the way out of town. "Thought I'd show you around. Hammond's probably changed a lot since you were here last."

Lee tried to avoid reading anything negative into his remark, tried not to infer an intended jab about the four-year gap between visits. She eyed the buildings as they slowly drove by. On her arrival in town, she'd been in too much of a dither about being late for the funeral to notice anything.

The truth was that the town looked about the same in reality as it did in her memory. The Doughnut Palace still stood on the corner, Bascomb's Antiques next door. And farther down, the big white auction barn. There was a new boutique called Alma's just on the fringes of the community. Other than that, everything seemed as it was four years ago.

"Well, that's it," Allen said, as they passed the city-limits sign and sped up. "You didn't blink and miss anything, did you?"

"No, I think I saw it all."

Lee felt a momentary sense of peace. It was comforting to return to a place where rapid change was not the order of business. In New York, something was always going up or coming down. Here, there was a kind of permanence, and despite her big-city bias, she had to admit Hammond had its way of easing into one's senses.

The Catfish Cabin was a rustic restaurant on the Ouachita River, the facade a graying cedar. Inside, tables covered with red-checked oilcloth were arranged in a hodgepodge fashion. Windows spanned one wall and twinkling lights revealed a pier stretching over the river.

"Hello, Allen." The waitress greeted them with plastic-encased menus.

"Hi, Peggy." He took both menus and laid them on the table beside him. "Is the beer cold?"

"Isn't it always? How about a pitcher?"

"That'll be fine. And we'll have the special."

Lee turned to Allen as the waitress left. "Thank you, Mr. Hilliard, for your courtesy," she said sarcastically. "Don't I even get to choose what I eat?"

"Trust me."

Lee rolled her eyes to the ceiling. There it was again. *Trust me.* What was he trying to do, convince himself? "That'll be the day. But since I'm apparently having it for dinner, just what is the special?"

"Fried catfish, French fries, red beans, coleslaw. Oh, and hush puppies, too."

Lee was familiar with Southern food from her business trips through Virginia, the Carolinas and Georgia. She liked different cuisines and generally tried to seek out the local specialties, but she had to protest Allen's suggestion. "My word, that's a whole week's worth of calories." She shook her head as the waitress appeared with a pitcher of beer and two ice-frosted glasses.

"I don't think a few calories will hurt you. From where I'm sitting, you look to be in pretty good shape."

"Oh, I don't know about that. Remember the saying, 'You can't be too rich or too thin.'"

"I remember it," Allen said. "I just don't happen to agree."

"With which part, the thin or the rich?"

"Both." Allen picked up the pitcher and reached for Lee's glass. "It's just as unhealthy being too thin as it is being overweight."

"And the rich part?"

"Money can cause a lot of unhappiness."

"Only when you don't have it."

"Sometimes when you do," he said.

"Is that the voice of experience?"

Allen shrugged. "Ready for your beer?" He handed Lee her glass.

The meal was as fattening as Lee had feared, but delicious, and Allen was an entertaining companion. During dinner, he shared several stories about her childhood.

"Did you and my grandmother ever talk about anything except me?"

"Sure. The weather, baseball naturally, but one of her favorite topics was you."

"I see," Lee said, not really seeing at all. Despite the recent efforts at reconciliation, she still found it hard to believe Grandmother was ever that interested in her. For obvious reasons, her sense of trust in family had never been well developed. Yet Allen wasn't the only one in Hammond who'd indicated that Delia liked to talk about her. Lee supposed she'd never stop wondering about it. She dunked her last French fry into a blob of catsup, then looked at Allen. "Let's talk about something else. You, for example. When did you meet my grandmother?"

"Let me see. I think it was when my first homer sailed through one of her second-floor bedroom windows." He laughed. "Delia was a little upset. Made me come in and sweep up the glass, then fed me cookies and milk. I was about ten at the time."

"So your family lived in Hammond?"

Allen's grin faded. "My *family* consisted of a series of foster parents, all of whom were glad to get rid of me when I moved on."

The hurt came through so strongly, Lee almost felt Allen's pain herself. Perhaps that was why she was so attuned to him; he, too, carried childhood scars. Perhaps they had more in common than she'd supposed. But tonight didn't seem the right time for baring their souls. Tonight they were supposed to be having a lighthearted dinner, not psychoanalysis. She quickly changed the subject. "Have you always coached?"

"No," he said.

"What else have you done?"

"Well, I've always been involved in baseball. Since I was knee-high to a grasshopper. But this is my first time as a coach." He poured the remains of the beer into their glasses.

"I repeat the question, then," she said. "What else have you done? Since you appear to know everything about me, it seems only right I know something about you."

"Since we're roomies, hmmm?" His ready smile returned as he picked up her hand and gave it a squeeze. His touch was like electricity, but Lee dared not show him the effect it had on her. She let her hand lie limply in his.

"I've done this and that," he answered, tracing a line on the back of her hand with his forefinger. "Mostly I've been involved in baseball."

"Come on now, out with your life story." She tried to pull her hand away but he tightened his grip.

"Yours is so much more interesting. Take this, for example...." He fingered the diamond solitaire of her ring. "Why are you marrying a man you don't love?"

Lee yanked her hand from his. "Just what makes you think I'm not in love?"

"It doesn't take a genius to figure that out. There are clues by the handful. First, most women in love sprinkle the name of their adored throughout the conversation. You've yet to even mention the mystery man."

"Michael."

"That's the first time the guy's name has come up since you arrived."

"I've only been here two days," she said.

"Most women would've mentioned Mitchell—"

"Michael."

"Yeah, most women would've mentioned Michael ten, twenty, maybe a hundred times by now. I'll bet you've never even slept with him."

"That does it. I've had quite enough of this conversation." Lee got up from the table and grabbed her bag, giving Allen a look of disgust. Then she headed for the door. "Is it possible to get a cab out here?" she asked the cashier.

Allen caught up with her and threw his arm around her shoulder. "Lovers' quarrel," he explained to the cashier and several customers waiting in the lobby. "Come on, darling, be a good girl now."

Lee was so dumbfounded she meekly went along as he steered her out of the restaurant.

LEE TAPPED HER FOOT impatiently while Allen opened the front door. She pushed past him, almost running for the staircase. Fury had ignited like an out-of-control forest fire during the silent drive home. How dare he take advantage of her vulnerabilities? How dare he intuit the very reasons she'd begun to question her relationship with Michael? How dare he conceal all but a shred of information about himself? How dare he...appeal to her...make her so aware...make her feel so sensual? She hated being this conscious of him. Allen Hilliard was insufferable!

Allen's hand caught Lee's just as she reached the first step. He turned her so that they were eye to eye. He had to know she was furious; there could be no mistaking her anger. But he also seemed to know the other thoughts spinning through her mind.

His brown velvet eyes entreated her to forget being mad, to forget everything but this attraction between them. His lips moved to hers. He was in command, a masculine, controlling force. They weren't equals in this game. Lee was the puppet, Allen the puppeteer, pulling all the right strings. She wanted to retreat, push him away. And she would...soon. For now, she reveled in the expertise of his lips as they moved over hers, teasing, testing, probing. She wanted more of his loving. She didn't want to listen to the voice of caution that intruded on her senses. What was going on here, that voice was saying. Why was she allowing this? The voice grew stronger and she pushed Allen away. "E-e-nough," she stammered.

"No," he answered, "not nearly enough." His lips descended again to hers. Lee turned her head, preventing him from kissing her again. His lips grazed her ear, then began nuzzling her neck.

Lee pulled back. This was just a game to him, not the fully emotional, deeply sensuous experience it was to her. Lee knew the kind of man Allen was. That aside, she *was* engaged—even if she was having strong second thoughts. "I want you to stop."

"That's not what your body is telling me."

"Then you're not listening very well." She moved up another step of the staircase, putting some distance between them. "Despite what your overstuffed ego is saying, I'm not interested in a romantic interlude with you. I don't even like you. I'm afraid you're just going to have to admit the mighty Casey has struck out."

"There's nine innings in a baseball game. Casey'll have another time at bat." He leaned against the banister, smiling that confident smile of his.

Again Lee was speechless. She opened her mouth, then closed it, before turning and darting quickly up the stairs to the safety of her own room.

LEE CREPT BAREFOOT down the stairs. Suddenly she felt silly. What did she think she was doing? Sneaking around wouldn't protect her from seeing Allen. He lived here; sooner or later she was going to have to face him again. Anyway, what difference did it make?

She'd soon be back in New York, and with luck, the only further encounter she'd have with Allen Hilliard would be through her lawyer. She'd have to check with Hubert Parker about the possibilities of eviction. She wanted the man out of her life.

She was surprised to discover that Allen had already been down to breakfast, though there was no sign of the man himself. Coffee simmered on the burner, and the newspaper—if one could call that ten-page document a newspaper—was unfolded on the table. She stared at it and thought how much she would give right now for a copy of the *New York Times*. Sunday to her meant the *Times* and a leisurely half-day savoring page after page of news and reviews. The *Hammond Herald* laid out in front of her could be disposed of in half an hour—if one read slowly. It was definitely not an event like the *Sunday Times*.

Lee read and sipped her coffee along with bites of powdered doughnut from Allen's opened box on the counter. Aside from the meals Rose cooked for him and his restaurant dinners, he seemed to subsist on a steady diet of junk food—cookies, corn chips, candy bars. Lee wondered how he stayed in such fine fettle. This was the same person who had the nerve to criticize her frozen TV dinner?

Where was he anyway? Not that it mattered to her, but he was certainly being quiet; he'd probably gone back to bed. She'd heard him drive off last night after she went upstairs. No telling what time he returned home. Obviously the poor man needed to sleep in mornings, what with getting so little rest at night.

Lee straightened up the kitchen, rinsing out her dishes, as well as Allen's coffee cup, and wiping up the powdered sugar trail he'd left. Then she went into the next room to resume her job of sorting and packing. Tomorrow, as soon as she saw the lawyer, she would be leaving, so all her decisions about Grandmother's things had to be completed today. Might as well finish off the dining room before tackling the living room.

Lunchtime rolled around, and still the house remained silent, except for the noises Lee made wrapping and boxing. She paused for a glass of milk, then curiosity began to get the better of her, and she climbed the stairs to Allen's bedroom. She placed an ear against the door. No snoring, no sounds of deep breathing, nothing. She knocked softly, then more vigorously but got no response. Gripping the old porcelain knob, Lee twisted it carefully and slowly opened the door. She stuck her head in and peered into the room.

Allen wasn't there. At least, she supposed he wasn't there. Hard to tell with all the mess and clutter—a towel tossed onto the rug, clothes piled in a corner, cleated shoes in front of the dresser and a shirt draped over the dresser lamp. In short, the room was a mess. And its occupant definitely was gone. Lee would have guessed he'd spent the entire night out if the dregs of morning coffee hadn't told her otherwise.

She ventured into the room. Hmmm. From what she could see of the furnishings under the clutter, they were decidedly masculine. He must have brought them to Hammond himself, because they certainly didn't match Grandmother's decorating style. The unmade bed sported a tufted black bedspread and a black laminated headboard with matching dresser. A black leather Eames chair sat in one corner, next to a chrome floor lamp. This was definitely not a quaint country room.

Lee spotted a photograph on the dresser and couldn't resist checking it out. It was not of a woman, as she had assumed, but of a younger Allen—five, ten years maybe—and another man, both wearing what looked to be University of Arkansas baseball uniforms, both with an arm around the other's shoulders.

Lee picked up the photo, wondering who this friend might be. Obviously it was someone special, special enough to be displayed in a bedroom, but there was no way to satisfy her curiosity. If she asked Allen, she'd have to admit to snooping around. The realization that she was, in fact, invading his privacy spurred a guilt reaction and she quickly moved toward the door and out of the room.

She descended the steps and headed back to her boxes. Where was Allen? She wondered if he was deliberately avoiding her. If he'd slunk off somewhere to prevent more close encounters like last night, to protect himself from another rejection. Probably—the coward. All talk and bluff at night, and in the daylight fainthearted. *What am I complaining about?* she suddenly asked herself. Hadn't she behaved the same way earlier? She was beginning to feel confused. Maybe attention to work would keep her head straight. She began carefully pulling out cups and saucers of a Wedgwood dinnerware set and placing them on the dining-room table.

It was nearly four when the back door burst open and Allen appeared, followed by three teenagers. They

were talking animatedly, stopping short when they saw
Lee.

"Hi," she said.

"Oh, guys—" Allen turned to the boys "—I don't
think you've met Lee—Mrs. Martin's granddaughter.
Lee, meet Mouse and Jason and J.B."

"Hello," they said in unison.

"See what we did today? It looks like good eating
tonight." Allen held up a string of the most disgust-
ing fish Lee had ever seen, all slimy and dirty-looking.
Of course she'd never really seen fish before, except
neatly filleted at the market, or on a plate surrounded
by lemons and parsley.

She could even smell the dreadful things from across
the room. "Are those really edible?"

"Not just edible, they're delicious. Prettiest string
of bass we've caught in some time. You're in for a real
treat."

"Yummy, I can hardly wait." She watched as the
four males sauntered over to the counter and dumped
the fish into the sink.

"Which one of you guys wants to do the gutting?"
Allen turned to Lee. "You may want to come and ob-
serve this—in case you ever have to clean your own
catch."

Lee felt a wave of repulsion at the spectacle over by
the sink. "If it's all the same to you fellows, I think I'll
return to my packing." She hurriedly left the room
before she was witness to more than she cared to see.

Talk and muffled laughter kept coming from the
kitchen for the next hour. Obviously bass cleaning was
big sport here. Soon the aroma of fish frying began to

assail her senses—a heavenly, inviting smell. Then Allen appeared at the door. "Why don't you join us?"

Lee was too hungry to resist. She was pleasantly surprised as she entered the kitchen to see that the table was set and that a spread of fried fish, hash browns, sliced tomatoes and iced tea awaited her. She turned to the boys—she noticed only two of them were here—and said, "It looks very nice."

As all four of them took chairs, she asked. "What happened to...?"

"Jason," Mouse prompted. "He works at Miller's Gas Station on weekends. Coach takes him home after work."

Lee wondered if that was the reason Allen had left last night. Why did that notion seem so much more appealing, she wondered, than the possibility of a late date? She certainly didn't care if he'd met a girlfriend, did she?

The other two boys, who were brothers, apparently didn't have to be home for supper. They seemed quite comfortable eating here, and it was obvious they had a special feeling for Allen and he for them.

During the conversation it became evident that the brothers' home life was something less than perfect. It didn't take much detective work to figure out that the father wasn't around and that the mother was too busy entertaining male guests to have much time for her sons.

Lee, a child of divorce herself, felt her heart go out to these youngsters. She knew the sensation of being shut out, of becoming an outsider in her own home. From the time her mother had divorced Lee's father and married Tim Benners, Lee considered herself a third wheel, odd man out. The couple was so close and spent so much time together, there didn't seem to be room for a child in their life. They even went to their deaths together in France. Lee mourned her mother's death, but in reality, she had lost her years earlier.

Seeing Allen giving of himself to these teenagers made her reevaluate her opinion of him. Much as she would prefer to label him a no-account slug, the man appeared to have some redeeming qualities. The adoration on those young faces told Lee that Allen Hilliard had another side to him.

When the meal was over, Allen shooed the boys off. "I know there's some homework waiting for you two. Now get along."

"No big deal," they said.

"I mean it," he answered. "I'm not going to have Miss Peoples chewing me out tomorrow because I kept you from studying your history lessons. Now get!"

Reluctantly the boys departed. Lee and Allen watched them as they left by the back door. Then they stood silently looking at one another. The quiet became embarrassing.

"You're good with the boys."

"I like kids. Those two are super—just need a little discipline."

"Like fishing?"

"You can teach a lot out on the lake. Wish I'd had someone around to take me fishing when I was their age," he said. He walked over to a stack of boxes and glanced back at her. "Are you all packed?"

She shook her head. "I've got a couple of boxes upstairs to finish before I go to see Mr. Parker tomorrow. What are your plans?"

"For what?"

"The future...you know. Where do you plan to live, with Grandmother gone?"

He cocked an eyebrow. "Maybe I'll come back to New York with you."

Why did her heart skip a beat? She knew Allen was only teasing. "What about the baseball team? What about the State Championship?" she managed to ask.

"That would be a problem," he admitted. "I guess you'll just have to stay here." He had crossed the room, closing the gap between them.

"I couldn't do that." Lee's eyes were held captive by his. "I'm strictly a city girl."

"Do they do this in the city?" His lips gently nibbled at hers. "Or this?" His mouth covered hers, coaxing her lips apart to deepen the kiss. Lee's arms crept around him. Why did he make her feel this way? In the distance she could hear the ringing of the telephone, but it didn't matter. She didn't want to break apart from Allen. His arms felt so good, so strong.... She felt suddenly bereft when he ended the kiss to move to the telephone.

"Hello. Well, hi, Mitchell. Sure, Lee's here. Lee, Mitch's on the phone."

Lee took the receiver from his hand. "Hi, Michael," she said breathlessly, glaring at Allen.

Allen grabbed a magazine from the counter and went outside to sit in the wooden swing on the back porch. Through the screen door Lee could see him loosen the top buttons of his shirt and kick off his tennis shoes. Despite his nonchalance, she knew he could monitor the phone conversation, could hear every word, from his position outdoors.

"That was Allen," Lee began. "He lives here…with Grandmother—he was her boarder. I couldn't just kick him out on the street, could I? What? Oh—" She lowered her voice "—kind of old…and fat…thinning hair, with a shiny bald spot."

She saw Allen's hand go to the crown of his head as if double-checking his hair. But Michael seemed to believe her. His voice, which had been formal and icy, was now beginning to defrost. Why was she lying to him? she wondered. Michael trusted her. Of course, up until now, he'd never had reason not to. They chatted for a few minutes longer, then hung up, Lee promising to call when she got home.

Allen strolled back into the kitchen as she put down the receiver. "Old? You're lucky I didn't come grab the phone and tell Michael his ladylove was giving him the runaround." He took her hand and ran it across his full head of hair. "Not bald—and no fat, only muscle." He moved her hand down his rib cage.

Lee's body began to react to this forced exploration. She told herself angrily that she shouldn't be feeling this way—and only moments after talking to Michael, yet. "Let me go," she ordered.

"Oh, no. I can't let that description go unchallenged." He pulled her tighter against him. "I think this old man deserves an apology, don't you?" he asked, kissing her forcefully, his lips so hard on hers she could barely breathe, his fingers wrapped around her arms like bindings. The kiss enraged her, yet excited her, too. It wasn't easy, but she garnered all her strength and willpower and pushed him away.

"That's quite enough," Lee said, her voice calmer than she felt. "I have to get back to my packing." She hurried from the kitchen, feeling a sense of relief that she'd escaped. It had been a close call.

LEE'S INDEX FINGER traced down the *P*'s in the small telephone directory. There it was, "Parker, Hubert, Attorney-at-Law." She glanced at the teapot-shaped clock on the wall. Nine o'clock. Surely Mr. Parker would be in his office by now.

"Good morning, Leanna. I was going to call you later on, soon as I got situated. Why don't you come in around noon?" he said. "That'd be the best time for Allen to get away."

"Okay," Lee mumbled, and hung up the phone. Allen? Why did Allen have to be present for the reading of the will? There could be only one answer—he must be included in it. Then it dawned on her. He'd probably charmed her grandmother into leaving something to him, maybe one of her heirlooms. Lee felt an unpleasant suspicion begin to surface. Oh, well, she couldn't worry about that now. There was too much work left to be done.

Two hours later, the rental car was loaded with her luggage and numerous boxes packed with mementos. After seeing the attorney, she planned to stop by the post office and mail most of the boxes to her apartment in New York. She knew it would be impossible to take more than one or two on the plane.

Lee walked back to the house for a last look around. She felt an emptiness, a sadness that was bittersweet, as she contemplated the living room. She would never be in this place again; Grandmother was gone, now the house. Farewell forever to Hammond, and no more

Allen. Somehow, she was surprised at the renewed sense of loss that invaded her wary heart.

She studied the furniture. A couple of the pieces would fit nicely in her apartment. Disposing of the rest was still a concern, but Mr. Parker would know what to do. And what was the best way to deal with Allen Hilliard? Would he want to stay put until the house was sold? Or might Allen be interested in buying it himself? If he could afford it. That fancy car he drove made her wonder if he was living above his means. Did his coach's salary provide enough for luxury sports cars?

LEE WAS SITTING in a leather wing chair at one corner of Hubert Parker's desk, Allen in an identical chair at the other corner. She stole a quick glance at him. He was wearing chinos and a short-sleeved yellow knit shirt; his face was solemn. He looked out of place, uncomfortable.

"'To my granddaughter, Leanna Elizabeth Martin, I bequeath all monies after my just debts are paid. I also leave to her any of the furnishings and keepsakes in my home, located at 216 Elm Street, Hammond, Arkansas, that she wishes to have.'" Hubert Parker paused, then turned a page of the crisp white legal document.

"'To Allen Hilliard, I leave the house and adjacent property located at 216 Elm Street. I also—'"

"What?" Lee's shocked voice interrupted the reading. She rose to her feet, her legs wobbly. All those lonely feelings that had started to abate—that had been soothed just being in Delia's home, reliving old memories—now returned in full force. No wonder she'd been so hesitant about completely trusting Grandmother. That house was the last link to her family and her past—and Grandmother had left it to Allen! He had usurped her role as grandchild, had taken her rightful place. Rejection surged through her body. She felt so hurt, so betrayed.... It just couldn't be. "There must be some mistake."

"There's no mistake, my dear," the lawyer's voice soothed. "Delia made this will only a few months ago. She was quite specific about its provisions."

Lee turned to glare at Allen. "So that's how it is! Well, I hope you're proud of yourself. Ingratiating yourself with my grandmother. Sweet-talking her out of her home! You made her trust you, then you cheated—"

"Just a damn minute!" Allen jumped up from his chair. "I didn't cheat anyone. I'm as surprised about this as you are. I didn't know Delia planned to leave me the house, did I, Hub?"

The lawyer shook his head. "Not as far as I know."

Lee ignored the lawyer. "Hah!" she said to Allen.

"Boy, you're one suspicious female. And greedy, too. Is that the reason you rushed down here? Just because you thought you were going to inherit a little property?"

"How dare you!"

"I dare just fine. You started this ugly discussion and I intend to put in my two-cents' worth. We haven't seen hide nor hair of you in years, but you arrive on the first plane after Delia's death. And once here, you can't wait to meet with her lawyer."

"I don't have to take these accusations. Who's this *we*, anyway? Who asked you to involve yourself in her life—in my life? You're the unscrupulous one in this room."

"Children. Children." Hubert Parker rose to his feet as he tried to calm them. "Do you wish to contest the will, Leanna?"

"Contest? No, of course not." She turned to stare at the lawyer. "I'm sorry, Mr. Parker," Lee said. "I'm sure my grandmother had her reasons for...for everything. And I don't intend to question them. I was just a little surprised, that's all." She took a deep breath. "There are probably a couple of details we still need to go over, but I really don't think I want to deal with them now. I'll just run back by the house for a few minutes, then I'll be on my way. I'll call you from New York later this week." Lee grabbed her bag and rushed toward the door of the office.

Allen reached out and grasped her arm. "Lee, we need to talk about this. Please."

She didn't respond. Instead, she glared silently at Allen's hand until he removed it. Then she continued her exit from the office.

Lee sat in the car in front of the house, tears streaming down her face. She couldn't stop them, and she didn't quite know why she was crying like this. After all, she'd learned her lesson years ago. She had no family, not really. She was alone, independent. And she liked it that way. No ties that bind...and chafe. She had her career; she didn't need roots. She'd grown up just fine without them.

Why did it hurt so much, then? The same way it hurt when she was a schoolgirl and no father appeared for the father-daughter dance. The same way it hurt when her mother was too busy flitting around the world with Tim to bother with a teenager on spring break.

Most holidays had been spent with school friends, the ones whose parents never minded an extra kid over Thanksgiving or Easter. Christmas generally meant the home of a faculty member. Something would always come up with her mother and stepfather, and Lee would hear the oft-repeated, "I'm sorry, darling, but we're unable to get back to the States." And from her father or grandmother, nothing. There were no cards, no letters, no invitations to spend time in Hammond.

It was as though Lee hadn't existed for Delia—until more than a decade had passed and Lee was grown, and her father dead. By then, she'd learned to do without family, to be self-sufficient. She'd gotten the message of rejection often enough in her life. Surely she was used to it by now.

So why the tears? It wasn't as though she wanted the house, she told herself. She didn't need it for the money. Not with her job and the income from her small trust fund. She turned off the car's engine and sat for a moment, gazing at the familiar white facade. Was she upset about losing the last remnant of her childhood? Lee wasn't sure where the misery was coming from, but she felt as though the rug had been yanked out from under her.

Reluctantly she dragged herself from the driver's seat. She opened the trunk and removed the largest box, then proceeded up the walk, plopping the box on the porch and turning back toward the car. As she walked along, she worked the house key loose from her chain. No need to keep this. She'd leave it for Allen.

"What are you doing?" Allen had pulled up behind her.

"Just what it looks like. I'm putting your things back."

"Don't be ridiculous. Delia left you everything in the house. She wanted you to have anything you cared about." He took the box from her arms and returned it to the trunk of her car.

"Did she? Or was it just a token gesture? The same kind of gestures I've had from my family all my life."

"Hey—" Allen brushed a tear from her cheek and peered into her face "—there's more to this than just the house, isn't there?"

Lee turned away. Then her anger came back and she shot him a hateful glance. "What do you expect from a greedy female like me? I'm crying over this vast estate I've just lost out on." Her tears dried as she snapped, "Now how about using a little of that brawn and helping me unload these? I don't want to miss my flight."

Allen shrugged and retrieved the large box from the trunk. "I'll mail these to you."

"Don't. I'll just return them."

"It's going to get pretty tiresome then, because I'll mail them back. Maybe we'll solve the problem of the post-office deficit—boxes going back and forth from Arkansas to New York ad infinitum."

"Do whatever you like," Lee said, too tired to argue anymore.

"We do need to talk about this." He looked at his watch. "But I've got a gym class waiting. Will you stay another day?"

She shook her head. "I've stayed too long as it is."

"Isn't there anything I can say to make you change your mind?"

"No." She handed him the house key and got into her rental car. She looked into the rearview mirror as the car rolled away. He was still standing in the same spot, watching her as she turned the corner.

CHAPTER FOUR

LEE LANDED at Kennedy Airport late Monday evening, bone tired after a two-hour delay in takeoff from Little Rock. The flight was bumpy as the plane skirted in and around heavy thunderstorms and only served to increase the tension she was already feeling.

The scene at the lawyer's office had cut her to the quick, had reopened old wounds. Lee was deeply distressed at this lapse into little-girl vulnerability; she had thought she'd developed a tougher hide after all these years. Her only option now was to put this whole unfortunate trip behind her and pick up her life where she'd left off.

But her reentry into New York was not without complications. For starters, she was greeted at her apartment by a rent-overdue statement under the door. In her haste to make her plane, she had forgotten to leave the check at the manager's office.

Her homecoming wasn't destined to improve. Lee dropped into a chair and slipped off her pumps as she reached for the "play" button on the answering machine. There were two messages—one from an obscene phone prankster and the other a curt, cold-voiced request from Michael to return his call "if you ever get home." After hearing his belligerent tone, Lee wasn't sure she didn't prefer the obscene caller. She reluctantly dialed Michael's number.

When he recognized Lee on the line his voice assumed the same icy tone she'd heard on the answering machine. She had half a mind to hang up. Desperately in need of comforting, she received none from Michael. Lee wondered how such a successful physician could be so totally lacking in empathy. Maybe he was different with his patients, she thought, but somehow she doubted it. Instead of providing the needed tea and sympathy, Michael conducted an inquisition about why the trip took so long, about the will and about "this Allen character."

Lee told him about the delay with the lawyer, gave only sparse answers about the will and avoided the questions about Allen. Once she'd hung up, Lee had to admit that his questions weren't unfair; really it hadn't been an inquisition. But sensitive as she was feeling right now, any inquiry concerning the will's contents was unwelcome. And she certainly didn't want to talk to Michael about Allen. When the call finally ended with a commitment for lunch the next day, Lee felt even more miserable than before, and she was relieved to escape a prolonged conversation with her fiancé.

"SO TELL ME about the trip."

"Do you want a minute-by-minute accounting of my time, or are you more interested in the inheritance?" Lee was seated across the table from Michael at the Tavern-on-the-Green. Her blue eyes were cold as she met his gray-eyed gaze.

Michael flinched. He set his water glass down. "That was uncalled for, Lee."

Lee shook her head as she apologized. "You're right. I'm sorry." It was foolish—and unjust—to punish Michael just because *she* was shouldering a painful rejection. She was going to have to stop being so touchy.

"I was hoping you'd be in a better mood today. I've got tickets for the opera tonight." He patted her hand as if consoling a sulky child.

"Just how good a mood would you be in if you'd received the welcome home I got from you last night?"

"You *were* gone five days."

"Well, it certainly wasn't a vacation. I had a miserable flight home, and talking to you didn't help a bit. Then today, I arrived at work to find my desk piled to the ceiling." Lee didn't mention her restless night; she'd tossed and turned for hours. She couldn't get Allen Hilliard off her mind. Especially since he'd called shortly after her conversation with Michael.

"Just wanted to make sure you got back okay," Allen had said.

"Well, you and your guilty conscience can relax. I'm here."

"Lee—"

She'd hung up on him. The phone rang again...and again. After fifteen rings, she knew Allen wouldn't give up. She reached behind the bedside table and pulled the plug, hoping to get a little sleep. Unfortunately, slumber eluded her until almost five in the morning.

As angry as she'd been at Allen—and she was furious—she also realized that, for the most part, he had been gentle with her, acting almost as though he knew she was hurt by the will. He knew and he cared.

"I should think all of that, and double—" Michael's voice brought her back to the present "—would be easier to face than the gunshot wound I had to deal with today in surgery. Emergency was overloaded and I had to step in."

Lee sighed. She understood that Michael's work was more important than hers, when you looked at the whole realm of things. She just got tired of being forever reminded how important it was—how important *he* was. She and Michael might not have the most romantic relationship in the world, but she'd always thought she cared for him, and that he cared for her, too. Now she was beginning to question not only her own feelings, but also Michael's. Wouldn't a man who loved a woman, even in Michael's restrained way, show an occasional glimmer of sensitivity?

Lee played with her salad. "I'm not trying to compare loan applications with life-and-death situations, Michael. I think you know that. Just the same, I would appreciate a little compassion on your part. It was a difficult five days."

"And I'm not helping, right?" Michael smiled as he phrased the question and Lee couldn't resist smiling back. She had to admit he could be charming when he put his mind to it. Too bad he had to put his mind to it. Being charming wasn't second nature to him, didn't come naturally to him like it did to...some men.

"So, are we on for the opera, Lee?"

"Oh, sure. Sounds fine," she said, giving him a weak nod and feeling less than enthusiastic. She was still tired—drained was more like it. She wished she could just retreat to her apartment and vegetate. But Michael wouldn't understand.

"Good girl." He stroked her cheek. "Getting out will help you get over your bereavement sooner."

Yes, she thought, *and maybe help exorcise unwanted thoughts of Allen.*

THE EVENING OUT DIDN'T HELP at all. Lee was optimistic at first when she discovered the opera was *Manon,* one she'd never seen before and wasn't familiar with. She hoped she could just lose herself in the story and the music—and give her mind a respite from the erratic, confusing, muddling thoughts that had been tumbling through it.

But try as she might, she couldn't avoid conjuring up visions of Allen as she watched the performance. For some ridiculous reason, every gesture and every nuance reminded her of him. She suspected that anyone else would have been hard put to find comparisons between eighteenth-century France and twentieth-century Arkansas, between the hero Chevalier des Grieux and Allen Hilliard. But Lee did. And the romantic scene in the last act evoked a melancholy that shocked her in its intensity.

Lee stole a peek at Michael. She realized she'd never felt the kind of love for him that the two singers swore for each other, and probably never would. She wondered if she actually possessed the capacity to care deeply. Love had not been a rewarding experience for Lee; on the contrary, it had guaranteed rejection every time. When Manon, the heroine, died in the arms of des Grieux, Lee felt a hot rush of tears. *Boy,* she thought, *I'm really wallowing in my misery these days.*

Michael looked her way. "No more operas with sad endings for you, my darling," he said. "Your red nose and mascara-streaked cheeks make you look like a sad-eyed clown." He reached into a pocket and pulled out a crisp white handkerchief.

"Thanks, Michael," she said bitingly, as she accepted the monogrammed hankie. "You always know how to bring me back to reality."

Michael laughed, apparently unaware of the rancor in her voice. "It's my medical training," he said. "Sometimes it gets in the way of sentiment." He rose from his seat, stepping into the aisle, and Lee followed. They headed toward the exit and out of the music hall. During the ride home, she couldn't keep her mind from wandering, reflecting on the difference in Allen's reactions to her tears. Remembering how his gentle kiss had cushioned her sorrow.

Michael rode the elevator up with her and walked her to the door of her apartment. "Why don't I come in for a nightcap?" He nuzzled her neck, but Lee gave only a token response before pulling away.

"Would you mind terribly, Michael, if we called it an evening? I'm so tired... I really would like to go to bed."

Michael hesitated for a moment, as though engaged in a silent argument with himself, before acquiescing. "Sure, darling. I'm being thoughtless. You get your beauty sleep and I'll see you tomorrow."

While Michael's good-night kiss was brief, it was also more demanding, more possessive, than ever be-

fore. He drew back to gaze into Lee's eyes, and she
wondered if he could read her thoughts, if he sensed
that she'd wanted to push him away, that her mind had
been on another man's kiss. Apparently not, because
he placed a second, softer kiss on her lips, then turned
and strode toward the elevators.

He was being surprisingly understanding all of a
sudden, she thought. For some reason she found his
familiar omnipotent-doctor personality, however irritating, easier to deal with than his occasional sym-
pathetic responses. She felt a sharp pang of guilt for
sending Michael away—and for spending most of the
evening thinking of Allen. Maybe she should have in-
vited Michael in, should have told him about her
doubts. How could she stay engaged to one man when
she was half in love with another? But were her feelings for Allen love...or obsession? She didn't know.
She only knew that the whole situation was making
her miserable.

LEE OPENED ONE EYE and glanced at the clock. Eight-
thirty. "Oh, no." She threw back the covers and rose
to a sitting position. Why hadn't the alarm buzzed?
She picked up the clock and studied the setting. The
alarm hadn't sounded because she hadn't turned it on,
that was why. The button was still in the off position.
Now she'd be late for work. She scrambled out of bed
and hurried toward the bathroom, unbuttoning the
top of her baby-blue pajamas as she made her way
through the door.

Thirty minutes later, she'd showered and half
dressed when the doorbell rang. She peeked through
the spy hole. It was United Parcel with a delivery. Lee

quickly pulled on her taupe suit skirt and high-collared white blouse. Had she ordered something from a mail-order catalog? She didn't remember sending for anything.

Four boxes were carried up to her apartment. She recognized them immediately; they were the same cartons she'd left in Arkansas. Allen had made good on his promise to forward them to her. She considered refusing delivery, but didn't have the time now to argue. She had to get to her office—her job didn't allow for five-day weekends and midmorning arrivals. Banker's hours were not as they appeared to other people, and Lee knew she was in for more than a few late evenings to compensate for her absence.

She slipped on her black pumps, grabbed her suit jacket and string of pearls and rushed for the door. She would worry about the boxes when she got home.

THEY WERE WAITING in her living room, right by the door where they'd been deposited, when she arrived home that night. She took off her suit jacket and pushed one of the boxes over to the couch, then decided just to forget the unpacking for now.

Her body felt limp, exhausted from the rush of the day and the emotion of the past week. She went to her bedroom to change clothes. Maybe a short nap would revive her, she thought, tossing her blouse and skirt over a chair and slipping into an old terry robe. Lee threw back the quilted comforter and stretched out on the bed.

The telephone rang. Seven o'clock. Michael. As predictable as ever. He always called after he'd completed his evening rounds.

But the caller wasn't Michael. "Are you going to be a coward and hang up again?"

Allen's challenge of "coward" did the trick. "What do you want?" she grumbled.

"To talk about the house. Lee, you can have it. I've already checked with Hub Parker. All I need to do is deed it over."

"For how much?"

"Listen, lady, can't you relate to anything besides dollar signs?"

"My apologies if I appeared ungrateful." Lee's voice was frosty. "But I'm no charity case, Mr. Hilliard. Keep the house."

"I can't win with you. Just what is it you want?"

"Nothing *you* can provide. Goodbye."

"No, not goodbye. Maybe what I can provide is exactly what you need. But you're too stubborn to realize it. See you around." The receiver clicked in her ear.

For the next several days Lee wondered if "See you around" meant Allen would show up on her doorstep. But one weekend passed, then two, and the threat of a visit faded. The boxes stayed in place, by the sofa and by the door. Lee had no time in her life to devote to the past. The present was too demanding. The bank she worked for had just merged with another, and the staff had been told to expect a lot of overtime.

And that was exactly what happened. Lee would work through her lunch hour, then drag home most nights at eight o'clock, nine o'clock, ten-thirty. There would be just enough time to eat a quick meal—a bowl of cereal or a cup of soup—decide what to wear the next day, then collapse into bed. Her few free evenings were spent with Michael. The cartons would just have to stay where they were for the time being. Besides, memories of the funeral and her trauma at losing her grandmother were beginning to soften around the edges, so she didn't feel as much need for reflection.

Until one Saturday afternoon, when Lee had finished a sinkful of hand washing, restocked her refrigerator and was taking a coffee break on the blue-flowered sofa in her living room. She sat on the couch, coffee cup in hand and eyed the boxes, still in their places, now almost accepted as part of the furnishings.

This was the time, she told herself, to get that clutter out of the living room, to put it away somewhere. She pulled a box closer to the sofa and reached for the scissors lying on the coffee table to cut open the top.

Inside were the linens from Grandmother's bedroom. She made three separate trips to her linen closet to distribute and arrange the sheets, pillowcases and towels on the shelves. One box down, three to go.

She opened another box. It contained the Wedgwood. Plates, cups, saucers—a full service for twelve. She took it into the kitchen. The dishes would have to be washed by hand; she didn't trust the dishwasher. But later, not now. She poured herself a second cup of coffee and went back into the living room.

The next carton was crammed with memorabilia—photographs and scrapbooks Lee hadn't had time to go through in Hammond. The pictures spanned three, four, five generations, subjects and dates all carefully noted on the back. Sepia portraits of Delia's parents, a few tintypes, a childhood picture of Great-Uncle

Claude, photos of Delia and her husband, Roy Senior,
holding their infant son, Roy Junior. Even some pictures of Lee's mother, Marie, taken right after she and
the younger Roy had married. They looked so much
in love. Lee felt sad contemplating how far they'd
drifted in the other direction, all the way to contempt
and loathing.

Lee set the pictures down on a side table and pulled
out a large album. The cover was handmade, a floral
needlepoint design. Probably Delia's handiwork. She
opened the cover and stared at the first page. It contained only one item—a copy of her birth announce-
ment glued to the middle of the page.

The next few pages were filled with Lee's baby pictures. There was a hospital photograph taken by a
professional, then snapshots of Lee in her bassinet, her
tub, her baby bed, being fed by her mother, being held
by Roy Senior. Some of the pictures Lee had never
seen. But after the pages devoted to Lee's early childhood, the photos began to fizzle out, which probably
coincided with the divorce. The rest of the album
contained only recent items Lee had sent herself—
shots of Lee and Michael on their ski trip last Christmas and a recent picture taken for a press release when
she'd been promoted to vice president. The cards and
notes she'd sent over the past few years had been kept
and added to this album. The last entry was the gift
card that had accompanied her flowers only months
before.

Lee sat stunned. Why had Delia Martin made the
effort of maintaining a scrapbook, a chronicle of the
fragile relationship with her granddaughter? What did
it mean? It certainly didn't mesh with the image of an

indifferent relative. Lee didn't feel she knew the answer, but for a few seconds, there was a kind of hope, a giddy sensation that someone else really had cared about her. Could this be true?

Soon reality began to assert itself. There were no answers to be found now. It was too late to speculate on her grandmother's motives—and what difference did it make, anyway? Grandmother was gone, Lee was alone, except for Michael, and she didn't have time to waste mourning what might have been.

She took the box into the bedroom, emptied the contents into two large bureau drawers and closed them. Only one box left. She would put the contents away, then begin preparing dinner. Today was Michael's birthday and she planned to make veal *cordon bleu*, his favorite dish. That would keep her hands and thoughts busy for the rest of the afternoon.

Still, Lee was anticipating the evening with mixed emotions. To a certain extent, she and Michael had settled back into their old relationship. Lee had tried to be more appreciative of Michael's attributes, had tried to look upon him as the sexy man her secretary, Maria, seemed to think he was. Every time Michael called, Lee got the same message over her intercom: "Dr. Gorgeous is on the line." Handsome, yes, but when Lee thought of sexy, her mind immediately pictured someone else.

Even though she hadn't heard from Allen since the day the boxes arrived, his image still burned in her brain. She had to forget him, had to concentrate on the man she was engaged to. Michael was subtly pushing her to set a wedding date. So far, Lee had been able to put him off. But eventually she would have to agree to a date or return his ring. She couldn't vacillate much longer. She wasn't up to talking about it tonight—but soon. Meanwhile, it was time to get dinner under way.

ALLEN WAS LEANING against the building when Lee walked out of the bank into the warm June afternoon. He looked almost as though he belonged on Wall Street. His shirt was crisp and white, his tie a blend of maroon and gray, a neat complement to the gray trousers, which perfectly fit his long, muscular legs. A navy blazer was flung over his shoulder, held in place by the index finger of his right hand. It was six weeks since she'd last seen him, but she spotted him instantly. "What are you doing here?"

"I'd have arrived sooner, but I had to wait until school was out."

Lee wanted to be annoyed. Instead she felt a tremor of excitement. She immediately wondered why he was in New York, and the adrenaline began to flow through her body.

He wore dark sunglasses that masked his eyes. "We've got some unfinished business...about a house in Arkansas."

"You're mistaken. That business is quite finished."

"Well then, maybe I need a loan." Allen pursed his lips in a tight smile.

"In that case, you're in the right place. But I'm afraid you're too late for business hours. Anyway—" she looked him up and down "—despite the dress-for-success look you're sporting today, I have my doubts about your reliability as a credit risk."

"You're not on your toes this afternoon, Ms. Martin. You're forgetting I have collateral," he said. "The house in Hammond."

"Oh, yes, how could I forget that?"

There was an uncomfortable silence, then Allen gave her a half smile. "Actually, as you well know, the reason I came was to see you."

His soft drawl and sexy grin caused another tremor to race through her body. Her heartbeat intensified. "We have nothing to say to one another," she answered, her voice shaky, uncertain. She looked up into his sunglasses, unable to read his expression.

"I think we do. We need to talk about the house, about Delia. Don't be so damn stubborn." He clasped her elbow. "I'll give you a ride home."

Lee was tempted. The heat and humidity were stifling on the busy sidewalk. Her green linen coatdress felt clammy against her skin. She dreaded facing a ride home on a crowded subway.

Allen must have caught her doubtful expression. He tightened his grip on her arm and steered her toward a white sedan parked on the street.

A typically audacious thing for him to do, thought Lee. Daring New York's finest. Not the slightest concern that he might get ticketed, or more likely, have his car towed away. He was acting as if he were back in Hammond. Find a place to park the car and just put it there; no tow-away threats or No Parking signs to cramp your style.

"I can't go with you," she protested, finally recovering her wits. She pulled her arm away.

"Sure you can. If you need to cancel something, we'll stop at a phone booth on the way."

"On the way where?"

"You'll find out."

"You've got something up your sleeve, haven't you? Well, Mr. Hilliard, I have no intention of going anywhere with you." She spun around to walk off, but Allen stopped her before she'd managed more than a couple of steps.

"It's your decision, lady. I've got some things to say—and you're going to listen. So take your choice. Come willingly, or I'll throw you over my shoulder and put you in the car."

"Try it, and I'll scream my lungs out!"

"Scream away. It'll make a nice little scene. If you scream loud enough, maybe we'll generate some publicity. Michael would love that."

"Leave Michael out of this."

"That suits me just fine—leave Michael out. Now which is it—willingly or over my shoulder? You've got to the count of three. One—"

"All right, you win." Lee knew it was time to back down. If anyone else had made such a threat, she'd know he was bluffing, but not Allen. He had enough gall to do exactly what he'd said. She got in the car without further argument, sitting mum in the passenger seat as they drove for more than an hour, finally escaping the busy traffic of the city and moving to the Atlantic shore.

Her curiosity began to get the better of her. "Where are we going?"

"We're almost there," Allen answered. Five minutes later he pulled the car into the parking lot of a luxury motel, bypassing the registration area and stopping in front of a side entrance.

"What do you think you're doing?" she asked irritably.

"It's not what it looks like." He switched off the ignition, then turned toward her. "I brought you here to talk."

"Oh, really? To talk? All these years I never realized that men brought women to motels for conversation." She sat with her arms folded, glaring out the windshield. "I have it on good advice that people are able to converse in New York City all the time."

Allen leaned his arm on the steering wheel. "That place has too many interruptions, no privacy. I wanted us to be together without a lot of interference."

"Well, that's too bad. I have no intention of getting out of this car and isolating myself with you in a motel room. You might as well turn around and take me back to New York."

Allen sighed. "Okay, maybe this wasn't such a great idea. Look, this place has a nice restaurant overlooking the water. Why don't we go get a drink? Maybe dinner."

She hesitated.

"Come on," he said. "You've come all this way. You might as well hear me out." He climbed from the car, then walked around to open her door.

She looked warily up at him. "We'll have a quick drink. Thirty minutes. No longer."

Moments later they were seated at a corner table in the restaurant, drinks in front of them—draft beer for Allen, white wine for Lee. Allen sipped his beer. "Nice view," he said as he glanced out the window.

"Surely you didn't bring me here to discuss the view."

"No." He grinned and she had to resist smiling back. "I guess I was just buying some time before I waded in."

Lee steadied the base of her wineglass with both hands. "So why don't you do us both a favor and get on with it."

"Lee, I want to talk about Delia."

"I can't see that there's anything else to say on the subject. Grandmother made her feelings perfectly clear." She raised her glass to her lips.

"On the contrary, she muddled things terribly. I know you were hurt. Delia wouldn't have wanted that. Neither do I. The only reason she left me the house was because she didn't want you to be bothered with an old small-town albatross."

"First you tell me you knew nothing about her leaving the house to you. Now you know her motive."

"Yes, I think I do. You probably can't understand this, but your grandmother and I developed a really close relationship."

"I can't understand?" Lee scoffed. "Obviously you were *very* close."

Allen's dark eyes took on an even darker cast. "May I finish?"

With a sigh, she lowered her gaze. There was no reason to be so belligerent. It certainly wasn't doing her any good to get upset again. And what did she have to lose by placating him? "Okay," she murmured.

"My return to Hammond was what you might call the prodigal coming home." He took a deep breath. "It was not the best of times for me—to say the least.

I was at loose ends. I bummed around town for a while, ate and slept very little, drank a lot. Then Delia offered me a room—and more. Best thing that ever happened to me. It was like having a mother and a grandmother and a friend all rolled into one."

"Where had you come from?"

"We'll talk about that later. Right now I just want you to understand how it was with Delia and me. Like I told you before, I grew up in foster homes around Hammond. Just passed from one place to another. Never did really have a home of my own."

"I think I can relate to that."

Allen stared quizzically. "How? You had a mother and stepfather. Other grandparents."

"My other grandparents died before I was born. Didn't Delia tell you? And my mother and stepfather had better things to do than allow an adolescent to interfere in their relationship."

He frowned. "But Delia told me what a good life you had—your mother marrying a wealthy guy who could give you both anything you wanted."

"Oh, sure." Lee's tone was biting. "Nice clothes. Good private schools. And the best servants to care for me in their absence—which was all the time."

Allen sipped his beer slowly. "I didn't realize. I'm sorry."

"Don't be sorry. As far as I'm concerned, that's ancient history."

"I'm not so sure," he said. "I think it still hurts you. And I also think Delia would have been very upset to discover your life was not what she thought."

"That's news to me," Lee said. "Delia never really cared about me or what happened to me. As a grandmother, she was a flop."

"Harsh words. Unfair, too. Look, Lee, regardless of how things seem to you, I'm convinced your grandmother was as much a victim of your parents' divorce as you were. You were her only grandchild, her pride and joy, until your father decided she shouldn't see you anymore."

"*My father?* It was my father's decision? Well, I guess I'm not surprised. He didn't consider me too important during the marriage. But cutting me off from Grandmother...why would he do such a thing?"

"I only know what Delia told me. He insisted they cut the ties, told Delia to forget you were his daughter."

Lee shook her head. "It's hard to believe—that he could be so misguided and that she could go along with it. Obviously wasn't a tough decision for her."

"Don't be too sure. Delia told me it was the hardest thing she ever had to do. But remember, Delia was a product of a different time. She grew up when the man was head of the household. In every sense of the word. She was conditioned to accept the man's word as law, even if the man was her son. Roy insisted it was the best thing for you if they eased out of your life."

"Best for me, or best for him?" Lee's expression held no softness.

"Who can say?" Allen shrugged. "Anyway, he convinced her it would be better if they eliminated regular contact. Said you'd be well taken care of by your mother and stepfather and that having two families, being shuttled back and forth, would only confuse you."

"My father was a fool."

Allen took her hand and she didn't object or pull away. "I don't think it was a decision that made anyone happy, Lee."

"It's really sort of funny." Lee gave an ironic laugh. "I felt like I had no real family. And he was worried about me having too much." She laughed again, weakly. "Isn't that the funniest thing you ever heard?"

Allen watched her through narrowed eyes. "No, Lee, I don't think it's funny at all. I think it's very sad. I didn't really know your father. But I do know you and Delia were kept apart when you both really needed each other. I call that a tragedy."

Lee felt her eyes start to tear. She didn't want to cry. Her memory flashed back to another time with Allen—a time when the tears flowed. It mustn't happen again.

Allen seemed to sense her turmoil. For several moments he watched her, saying nothing, his hand still gently resting on hers. Lee tried to turn her face away, but felt captured by his eyes. Finally he broke the spell. "Do you want another drink, or shall we take a walk?"

"Let's walk."

They left the restaurant and walked along the weathered boardwalk and down steps leading to the beach, Allen's hand steadying Lee as her high heels dug into the sand. They sat on a bench and silently watched the waves lap the shore. A streak of neonlike lightning snaked across the northern sky.

"It's going to rain," Lee said.

"Probably." Allen sat quietly for a few moments, gazing pensively out at the ocean. "You want to know the real reason I didn't go to Delia's funeral?"

She turned to him. "Why?"

He slipped his hands into his pockets. "I was scared I'd break down and bawl like a baby. I couldn't risk it. Delia would've understood."

Lee didn't know what to say. She focused her eyes straight ahead, aware he was watching her. "I appreciate your telling me that. If I'd realized at the time how Grandmother and I had been kept apart, I'd probably have joined you in creating a real spectacle." Lee felt as though she was babbling. Allen was too close, his sensitivity too appealing, his male virility too potent. She could hear his breathing, smell his cologne. "But there was really no need for you to come all this way."

"I tried to tell you on the phone. If you recall, you wouldn't listen."

"You could have written."

"Could I have written this?" His fingers clasped her chin and he gently tilted her head toward his. Lee wasn't sure whether it was thunder she was hearing or the pounding of her own heart. Firm, soft lips met hers. "Lee..."

CHAPTER FIVE

THEIR LIPS WERE PRESSED together for long moments before Lee pulled away. She couldn't allow this to go on. It was a betrayal of everything she believed in. "Please," she managed to mumble, "don't.... Stop."

"Don't stop—okay."

Allen's head leaned toward hers again, but she halted his movement with the palm of her hand. "You know that wasn't what I meant." She stood up and walked a few yards along the beach before easing down onto the sand, heedless of her work dress and sheer hose.

Allen followed quietly and sat down beside her. For minutes neither spoke.

Lee could stand the silence no longer. She eyed the flickering lightning again. "The weatherman's been predicting rain all week."

Allen nodded, but didn't respond.

Why was she uttering such inanities? Lee wondered. The weather wasn't what was occupying her mind.

She pulled off her shoes and sat primly, arms hugging her knees, toes pressed into the sand. She gazed blankly at the horizon. Dared she believe what Allen had told her at the restaurant? Even though she wanted to, it took a giant leap of faith to accept the theory that her grandmother was not uncaring, but was—like Lee herself—a hapless victim of Roy's and Marie's divorce. There were still too many doubts and *what if*'s to assimilate; she needed more time to reflect on the information she'd been handed by Allen if she was to understand her grandmother's actions.

Right now she felt more confused than ever. And not just about Grandmother. She was uncertain why Allen had come to New York, didn't know what his intentions and his motives were. He said he was here to see her. But why? Surely he realized there could be no future for them; after all, she was engaged to marry someone else. Yet when he kissed her. . . She had to make him stop kissing her!

Ever since she'd done just that and pulled away, Allen had been sitting next to her, quietly staring out at the water. Lee watched him from the corner of her eye.

His dark eyes were fixed on the distant horizon, his thoughts apparently somewhere else. What was he concentrating on so intently? Was he angry, hurt?

Lee wished she could see the thoughts behind that inscrutable, fixed stare. He'd done his civic duty, had shown true Southern chivalry by seeking her out to explain about Delia and offering to transfer title to the house. He could give himself a pat on the back for being such a Good Samaritan. So what was the most gracious way to escape his company? To tell him "thanks and so long"? No answer came. Unsure of what to say next, Lee rose to her knees and looked around for her shoes.

"Do you feel like walking?"

"I don't think so," she said. "We need to get back."

"We do? You've made plans for the evening?"

Lee glanced at her watch. "It's rather late now to worry about plans." No need to tell him Michael was out of town; that would only complicate matters further.

"Lee?" Allen touched her arm.

"Yes?"

"Don't marry Michael."

"What?" Lee looked at Allen incredulously.

"Don't marry Michael," he repeated. His body moved closer to hers. "There's something between us, Lee. Something we need to explore."

"Something between us?" So he felt it, too. But she couldn't act on that feeling—not while she was still engaged to Michael. Some serious decision-making was in order, but she couldn't do it here, not with Allen confusing her so. She needed some space.

Lee started to stand up, but Allen's reflexes were too quick, and his firm grip prevented her from rising to her feet. He pulled her down against him and his lips sought hers, grazing instead the nape of her neck as she twisted aside.

"Don't," she pleaded.

"You said that before."

"And I'm saying it again." Her resistance, however, was short-lived. Slowly, sensually, as though their movements had been choreographed, Allen turned her toward him and stared into her face, saying nothing. Then his eyes drifted shut as his head bent and their lips met. A long kiss, not rough, but intense and demanding. Lee felt the pressure of his chest against hers, heard the quickening of his heartbeat.

Had it not been early June, she'd have sworn it was the Fourth of July. Suddenly all around her, it was warm, wonderfully warm, and she sensed a hot rush through her body. The sand, which had been cool before, seemed to take on the heat of her skin through her dress.

Fireworks were beginning to explode inside her. As she opened her eyes, she saw that despite the threat of rain to the north, the stars, too, appeared to be bursting in the sky, illuminating the beach where they lay. She felt alive, in love. In love? With Allen?

Allen's voice intruded on her thoughts. "Can Michael kiss you like that?"

The question brought her to her senses. Lee jerked away, her sudden movement startling Allen into releasing her. "How dare you!"

"I'm sorry," he said. "That was stupid of me."

"Yes, it was." But Allen wasn't the only stupid one here. What did *she* think she was doing? A mature woman—a woman engaged to another man at that—sprawling on the sand fully clothed and making love like an out-of-control teenager. This was ridiculous, and worse, dishonorable.

Lee jumped to her feet and grabbed a shoe. Where was the other one? She looked around frantically. There it was, embedded in the sand where she had lain. She dug out the shoe and turned it upside down to empty it of sand, then tried to balance on one foot so she could slip it on.

"Here, I'll help you."

"Don't touch me," she warned, easing into the shoe, then heading purposefully toward the car. She couldn't get away from here soon enough. This man had unsettled her, made her act crazy. After a few paces, however, one of her heels sank deep into the sand, and with her next step it broke off. "Darn, now look what happened! My best pair of shoes."

"I offered to help you," he shouted.

She glared as he approached. "The only way you can help me is to take me home."

"Whatever you say." His eyes were dancing in the starlight. He pressed his lips together and quickly turned his face away.

Was he hiding a smile? *So help me,* she thought, *if he laughs, I'll kill him.*

Allen must have sensed the threat in her voice, because he followed quietly behind as she hobbled toward the car. Just as quietly, he slid into the driver's seat and drove out of the parking area onto the highway.

"Are you going to ride stone-faced the whole way back to the city?" Allen took his eyes off the road for a moment to look her way.

She gave him a sidelong glance that said yes, that was exactly what she intended to do.

"Lee, there's no use being upset, no use trying to pretend this thing between us isn't there."

"What 'thing'?"

"This attraction, this yen or whatever you want to call it. Our feelings for each other."

"What happened at the beach was an accident, a fluke," she said. "And it won't happen again. So I suggest you just forget it. Keep in mind I'm going to be married to Michael. Next month," she lied. She stopped. Now what made her do that? Lying was against her nature. But somehow it seemed justified.

She needed some breathing room, a chance to think. Allen was being too aggressive.

"Next month, hmmm?" He looked over at her again. "That doesn't leave much time."

"Time for what?"

"Oh, you know," he said. "Planning the wedding and all. I guess you're pretty busy right now, what with the preparations."

"That's right. Very busy."

"Too busy, I guess, to show an old friend the big city."

"Much too busy." Her mouth twisted derisively. "And if you're the 'old friend,' forget it. I'd just as soon escort Jack the Ripper."

"Jack the Ripper, huh? I assume that's not a compliment."

"You assume right."

"So you're willing to let a defenseless country boy from Arkansas feel his way around the big city all alone."

"Defenseless country boy?" She rolled her eyes. "Give me a break. Besides you seem able to get around okay without any assistance."

"Beginner's luck. But I need someone to show me the sights. You know, the Empire State Building, Statue of Liberty..."

"Well, if you want to see the sights, I suggest you sign up with a tour group."

"It's not the same," he said.

"As what?"

"As having a friend take you. Being cooped up on a bus with a bunch of strangers doesn't sound like fun."

"I'm sorry, but your fun is not my concern. And even if I had the inclination, which I don't, I haven't got time to play tour guide, what with my job—and the wedding plans," she remembered to add.

"Oh, come on," he said. "I showed you around Hammond, remember?"

"You mean that five-minute tour?"

"You saw the whole town, didn't you?"

"That I did."

"Well, then, you owe me. How about it? Just one day. Tomorrow. Surely that's little enough to ask. Delia would have wanted you to do it."

What a sneaky ploy, Lee thought. Trying to make her feel guilty to get his way. Well, it wasn't going to work. "Leave my grandmother out of this. The answer is still no."

"Would it help if I said please?"

"Read my lips. No, no, no."

"Is that your final no, no, no?"

"Count on it."

The car pulled up at her apartment building. She hurriedly opened the door to get out. "Good night," she muttered. "I'm sorry your trip here was a wasted effort."

"Don't worry about my trip being a waste," he said.

"Believe me, I'm not worried." She turned her back and walked unsteadily on her uneven heels toward the double doors. With as much dignity as she could muster, she nodded to Phil, the doorman.

She was relieved to finally get away from Allen. She'd almost fallen prey to his Neanderthal charms— again. She hadn't been to bed with a man since her marriage had ended, yet she came frighteningly close to making love with Allen whenever and wherever he wanted. Thank goodness she had stopped herself from completely losing control.

Lee took a deep breath and pressed the elevator button. She watched the doors slide open, wondering as she stepped inside why her relief was accompanied by a feeling of deflation. *I'm probably just tired,* she thought. *A long workday and an evening of mental tug-of-war. A couple of aspirin and a long bath are just what I need right now.*

Lee entered her apartment and gently closed the door. It was good to be home. Or was it? She didn't seem to be sure of anything tonight.

THE BATH AND ASPIRIN did not ensure a sleep-filled night, and Lee tossed and turned, plagued once again by images of Allen. She thought back to the beach and the surprise embrace, hating herself for the warm feelings it had evoked. She was beginning to think the decision she and Michael had reached—to tone down the sex and concentrate on the companionship—had been a mistake. Clearly her body was sending signals, messages of longing. The problem was that her body had confused Michael with Allen.

One thing was certain—she needed to make a decision about Michael. She'd wavered long enough. She had to clear her head, end this simpering and day-dreaming. She had more important things to do with her time; work, for instance.

There was plenty of that. Lee was grateful the next morning for a full in-basket spilling over onto her desk. She took off her navy suit jacket and hung it on the coat tree, sitting at her desk as she picked up the first folder.

Two hours passed and Lee was contemplating a cup of coffee when Maria knocked and entered her office. "Lee, Mr. Stone wants to see you. He didn't say why."

Lee looked up. "Okay, thanks." She marked her place in the file with a paper clip, then slipped on her jacket. "He probably wants an update on the Malcolm Properties foreclosure."

She walked down the thick-carpeted hallway to the senior vice-president's office and knocked.

"Come in."

Lee opened the door, smiled at Donald Stone, then froze, her mind refusing to accept what her eyes were seeing. Allen was sitting to the right of the large mahogany desk, smiling what she'd heard someone in Hammond refer to as a possum-eating grin. Lee could have happily slammed the door and run back to her office, but instead she walked compliantly over to her boss's desk.

"Lee, I believe you've met Allen Hilliard."

She nodded and gave Allen a tight-lipped smile. "Hello again, Mr. Hilliard."

"Allen has just opened a new account with us."

Lee was astonished. An account? Where in the world did he get the money? Especially the kind of money that merited personal attention from Donald Stone? The senior vice-president only concerned himself with customers in the million-dollar range. Her mind was abuzz—especially after Mr. Stone's next words.

"At the same time, he's made an unusual request, one I'm sure you'll be pleased to honor."

"Oh?" Why did she already know what was coming? She looked at her boss, a fixed expression on her face as she tried to hide the displeasure she felt. She should have known Allen wouldn't give up so easily.

"Yes," Mr. Stone continued, "Allen indicates he's going to be in the city for a few days and he'd like to see the sights. Since you two have already met, he asked if you might be available to escort him. Are you available, Lee?"

Lee thought back to her overloaded in-basket, to the extra evenings she'd have to put in to make up for the time off. But what could she say? Mr. Stone seldom requested that she entertain a client, and he'd asked her in front of Allen. There was only one obvious response. "Yes, I'd be happy to show our guest around," she said. Did her words sound too forced? No, Mr. Stone looked convinced.

"Great. It's on the bank, of course. Perhaps you might try dinner at that new place in the Village everyone's been talking about."

"Dinner?"

"I hope there's no inconvenience there." Donald Stone smiled, clearly not caring whether she was inconvenienced or not.

Allen was due for a surprise if he thought she was going to be maneuvered into dinner, too. "Oh, I'm so sorry," she said, giving him a butter-wouldn't-melt-in-her-mouth look, "but I've already got a commitment for the evening. I'm on the planning committee for the Crystal Charity Ball. Tonight's our final meeting before the Friday gala. What a pity."

"No problem. Dinner tomorrow's fine with me," Allen volunteered. "I'm going to be in town for a couple of days."

"Tomorrow then?" Mr. Stone turned to her. "Okay, Lee? I believe you said Dr. Dayton is in London until Thursday."

Why on earth had she shared that personal tidbit? Now she was trapped. She knew that Mr. Stone would be extremely annoyed if she found another excuse to avoid dinner. "I'll have Maria make reservations," Lee said to Mr. Stone. "I'm sure we'll enjoy the restaurant you suggested."

Only Allen caught the irritation in her voice as he shot her a quick wink, then grasped Donald Stone's hand in a hearty shake. "Thanks, Don."

"Anytime, Allen."

Don? Allen? What had come over the aloof Mr. Stone? His long, taciturn face was almost radiant. Lee had never seen him show a client such deference and animated attention. You'd have thought Allen was an Arabian prince come to deposit all his oil holdings. Yet Allen's only apparent asset was his sports car—a purchase that probably had taken a big chunk of his pay check. This whole scenario didn't make sense.

Allen and Lee walked out of the office and into the hallway. "Congratulations," she said. "I don't know how you managed this, but it looks like you won, after all."

"Oh, you're not going to be a sore loser, are you?" He reached out to take her arm, but she pulled it away.

"I may have to be your tour guide, but I don't have to pretend I like it. Where to first?" she growled.

"Wherever you say. You're the boss."

"You could've fooled me." Her eyes narrowed as she tried to read the expression on his face. It wasn't hard to do. All that was missing were the canary feathers sticking out of his mouth. She hadn't believed it possible, but the more she saw of him, the more insufferable he got. "Follow me," she said. "I need to grab my purse and tell Maria I'll be out for the rest of the day."

"After you," he said, gesturing her to lead.

Allen followed her down the hall to her office, passing Maria's desk on the way in.

Maria looked up, then stared at Allen as though he were Superman just arriving by air and leaping in from the ledge. Her lips parted in surprise, and her eyes widened. *She must be more hard up for a man than I realized,* Lee thought, as she studied Maria's undisguised reaction to Allen. Sure he was good looking—but not *that* handsome. Maria was definitely overreacting, Lee tried to convince herself.

Allen seemed to savor the attention, casting a brilliant smile Maria's way. Deciding to call a halt to the mutual adoration going on, Lee hastily grabbed her purse and gestured Allen out. They made their way down the elevator of the high-rise building and onto the street. Lee looked around. "Where's your car?"

Allen pointed to a nearby taxicab. "I thought a taxi'd be easier to get around in than the rental car. This is Max." Allen introduced her to a mammoth man who was slouching against the cab smoking a cigarette. "He's ours for the day."

Lee said hello to the burly cabby, who straightened up at their approach. He nodded cordially in return. "Pretty sure of yourself, weren't you—lining up a cab," she muttered to Allen. What in the world had Allen offered him? New York cabdrivers didn't come cheap. And thank goodness they didn't come by the pound. She turned to the rotund Max as she opened her purse. "What's your fee for the day?"

Allen's brown eyes flashed in annoyance as he stopped her from removing her wallet. "Max's fee is taken care of. Put your money away and stop being so damn condescending."

Lee meekly closed her purse. She hadn't meant to put him down. "I'm sorry," she mumbled in embarrassment, "but Mr. Stone said..." She felt strangely close to tears.

His hand caught her chin and tilted it up as he saw the shimmer in her eyes. "Lee. It's okay. But I don't care what Don Stone said. As you well know, he was just a means to an end."

"I've never seen him act like that—so obsequious. How did you get him to agree to a tour?"

"Oh, it was nothing really. Just used the old Hilliard charm."

"Donald Stone doesn't respond to charm. Only dollar signs."

"Tsk, tsk," Allen clucked. "How you underestimate me and my winning ways. Now, no more discussion of your boss, okay?" Allen pulled away to open the car door for her and motioned her inside.

"Where to first, 'Batman'?" the driver asked. Max flipped his cigarette into a trash can and walked around to the driver's side.

"What did he call you?" Lee looked at Allen as they climbed into the car. "'Batman'?"

"I don't know," he said, shrugging. Allen leaned forward to speak to Max. "The lady's in charge. She'll tell you where to go first."

"Rockefeller Center," Lee said.

Max nodded as the taxi eased into traffic and sped off down the street.

By one o'clock they had covered Rockefeller Center, Lincoln Center, Grant's Tomb and were now at Central Park. Time for a lunch break. Lee had decided a hot-dog stand would be just the ticket for an authentic lunch in New York. If Allen thought they'd have a romantic tête-à-tête at some secluded restaurant, he had another think coming.

They stood on the street trying to eat the messy hot dogs without dribbling the contents down their clothes. Lee had gone for the basic dog with mustard and relish, but Allen had ordered the works—mustard, relish, chili, cheese, catsup, onions and sauerkraut.

"That concoction's going to eat the lining out of your stomach," Lee said as she wiped a smear of mustard from her lips.

"Me? No way. I always eat my hot dogs like this— a little bit of everything. I'm afraid I'll miss something if I leave off anything." He took another hearty bite.

"Aren't these hard to come by in Hammond?"

"Yes. So I manage to get away every now and then to the big city for a fix. Just like I'm doing now."

"Any special reason? Vacations? Business? Do you have something going besides high-school baseball?"

"Yeah."

"Well?" Lee prodded irritably. She was getting tired of his nonanswers.

"Vacations...business...a little of each."

"Tell me about the business part," she said.

"You don't want to hear about boring business matters, do you?"

"Boring? Not to me. Have you forgotten I'm a banker?"

He grinned. "As a matter of fact, I had. You look so pretty in the sunlight, I forget there's an executive beneath that gorgeous facade." Allen straightened the collar of her mauve silk blouse.

"I'm not sure whether to be flattered or insulted. I'm supposed to look businesslike, not gorgeous."

"Don't be insulted. Nothing wrong with looking both." He threw his napkin into the trash container and gave her a broad grin. "Besides I like to mix business and pleasure. Where to now, Tour Lady?"

Lee tried to ignore the jellylike feeling in her knees caused by Allen's flattery. She mustn't let him con her into submissiveness. "Well, we only drove by the Guggenheim. Do you want to go back and see it, or would you rather head for the United Nations and the Statue of Liberty?"

"The Statue sounds like fun. Maybe the Staten Island ferry, too. Ready, Max?" he yelled over to the cab.

Max lowered the newspaper he was reading. "Ready."

The weather began to change as the Staten Island ferry headed back toward the dock. Clouds had rolled in to blanket the sky and the air felt heavy with moisture.

"Looks like there's a downpour on the way," Max said as they scrambled into the cab. Big raindrops were already pelting the roof of the taxi.

"We'd better get this lady back home, Max." Allen rattled off Lee's address as if it were his own. By the time they arrived at her apartment, the sky was completely black and thunderclaps were resounding around them. The rain was falling in torrents.

Lee opened the cab door. "The weather's so bad, I'll just see myself inside."

"No way," Allen said. "I don't want you chastising me about my manners. Run on to the door and I'll follow you in."

The doorman smiled and tipped his hat as they entered the lobby. It was the first time Lee had seen Phil smile since she'd moved in three years before, but he greeted Allen almost like a long-lost friend.

They reached the elevator and she turned to him. "No need for you to come up. I'll just say good night here."

"Nonsense. I'd never forgive myself if I didn't see you all the way to your door. After you," he said, gesturing her inside the elevator.

Fortunately the elevator was occupied, by an elderly couple from the eighth floor who appeared just in time to board with them. Lee didn't like the idea of being alone with Allen in a small enclosure; she didn't trust him or her ability to control him—or herself, for that matter. Finally the car stopped at the seventh floor, and Lee and Allen got out and walked toward the door of her apartment.

"Well, I guess this is good night." She slipped the key into the lock.

"Aren't you going to at least offer me a towel to dry off with?" He ran his hand over his head, sending a spray of water through the air. "And a drink to warm me up on a night like this?"

"It's raining, not freezing." She hesitated. "Anyway, what about Max?"

"Don't worry about Max."

"Okay, a towel," Lee said.

"And a drink?" he prodded.

"Okay." She glanced at her watch, "Time for *one* drink."

Lee pushed open the door and stepped aside to let him enter. Out of long habit, she carefully locked the door again and put on the chain—something they probably didn't have to do in downtown Hammond, she thought wryly. When she turned around to face him, Allen's arms wrapped warmly around her, pulling her body to his.

"Allen, be good," she begged.

His lips pressed against hers, coaxing, teasing, urging. His mouth moved away slightly, and he murmured, "When he's good, he's very, very good."

"And when he's bad, he's horrid," Lee snapped, as she jerked free from his grasp. "If you pull another trick like that, it's a paper towel and a drink to go."

"All right, I'll be on my best behavior." Allen looked around the apartment. "Why don't I fix us both a drink while you get out of those damp clothes? Where do you keep the scotch?"

She gestured to the kitchen. "Liquor's on the right, glasses on the left, and soda in the refrigerator. Just a cola for me, please."

Lee headed toward her bedroom to change, pausing to switch off her answering machine and listen to the lone waiting message. "Lee, Grace Billings. The weather's frightful so we decided to put off the meeting until noon tomorrow. Hope that's okay with you. Call me in the morning."

"Well, what do you know about that."

Lee whirled around. Allen was still in the room watching her. His lips were curved in a satisfied grin, his brown eyes merry.

"I thought you were going to make a drink."

"I was—but I'm sure glad I decided to eavesdrop instead. No meeting means we can have dinner together, after all."

"No!" Lee's voice softened. "No. Michael may come over."

"Michael's in London."

"Oh, that's right...but still, I've got a million other things to do. In fact, it'd be best if you left now. Before the weather gets worse."

"You promised me a drink."

Lee started to protest, but her wet clothes were clinging to her body, and the idea of shedding her suit and panty hose and high heels seemed more appealing than an argument she'd probably lose anyway.

When she reappeared in the living room, Allen eyed her yellow cotton jumpsuit. "How do you manage to look demure and enticing at the same time?" He was lounging on her sofa, one arm draped across the back, the other holding a glass, and looking as though he owned the place. He'd removed his jacket and tie and partially unbuttoned his shirt. One of her kitchen towels was tossed over his shoulder. The man seemed to be at ease anywhere and everywhere, adapting naturally to new environments.

"I like the whatchamacallit." He gestured at the yellow-and-turquoise scarf she'd tied around her wet hair to keep it off her face. It was a different look from what Lee was used to. A look Michael would have hated—She stopped herself. She had to avoid mentally comparing the two. After all, there really was no comparison. The men were totally different. Why then, with all his admirable qualities—his sophistication, his intelligence—did Michael seem to be coming out second-best in her mind?

"Quit thinking." Allen was standing beside her. He reached for her scarf and adjusted it slightly.

Lee pushed his hand away. "What are you talking about?"

"Quit thinking so much. Let's just enjoy our drink." He handed her a glass. "I can hear those little wheels turning in your head. That may be the only thing wrong with you, Leanna Elizabeth. You're too damn smart. It gets in the way sometimes."

She frowned at him. "A few brains never hurt anyone."

"We're talking about more than a few," he returned softly.

Lee tried to frown a second time, but didn't quite pull it off. She was falling for his flattery again; she couldn't help herself. Most people commented only on her looks, as though they couldn't care less about her mental acuity. Even though she was a successful career woman, she still encountered the occasional person who implied she'd worked her way up the business ladder using her body, not her intellect. But Allen had seen more than the glamorous, sophisticated exterior. He was complimenting her mind, and she couldn't stifle a smile of satisfaction. "Where did you go to charm school, Mr. Hilliard?"

He laughed. "I said earlier that you underestimated me. But with you, that seems to come naturally. Anyway, since when does truth have anything to do with charm?"

She smiled again, then sat down beside him. Sometimes it was hard to remember that she didn't like Allen Hilliard.

CHAPTER SIX

ALLEN DRAINED his scotch and soda and clinked the ice in his glass. "That was just the ticket," he said. "Where's your telephone book? I'll order in some Chinese." He placed his glass on the coffee table. "Or would you rather go out?"

"In this weather?" Lee, who had been nursing a cola drink, set her glass down, too, and looked at her watch. "I don't think Chinese is a good idea, either," she said with a yawn. "It's been a long day and I'm really exhausted."

Allen grinned. "Are you trying to tell me something?"

"Only that I need to get to bed pretty soon."

"Now, that's the best idea you've had all day." He reached over and patted her knee.

Lee picked up his hand and dropped it onto his own knee. "I meant alone." She didn't have the energy for more verbal sparring.

"So much for good ideas." He moved to the telephone. "But you've still got to eat. Now, where's your telephone book?"

Lee pointed toward the bookshelf in the corner, then rested her blond head against the back of the sofa. What was the use of making a fuss? She had to eat; might as well let Allen order something. Her refrigerator was almost bare, anyway. Chinese food sounded better than a grilled cheese sandwich.

"But what about Max?" she asked. "Isn't he getting a little tired of waiting?"

"Oh, I let Max go." Allen frowned sympathetically. "Poor guy needed to get home to his family."

In less than thirty minutes the delivery boy from Suzie Wong's was at Lee's door. Fortunately for him, the storm had abated slightly. Still, the black umbrella the boy leaned against the wall deposited a wet puddle on the hallway's carpeted floor. Lee noticed Allen slip the youngster a ten-dollar tip in exchange for the large white paper bag filled with the familiar Chinese-food cartons.

An hour later the meal was finished. They'd dined in the living room, food spread out on the coffee table, Lee and Allen seated on cushions on the floor. It was casual and comfortable and they'd talked of this and that—Delia, sight-seeing, Lee's job. The conversation had been light and easy, relaxing.

They'd just started to gather up the remnants of their meal when there was a particularly violent flash of lightning, accompanied by the simultaneous crashing of thunder right outside the apartment window. Startled, Lee shrieked, grabbing Allen's arm in a reflexive motion. Without missing a beat, Allen responded by moving closer to her.

"Don't worry." He wrapped an arm around her shoulders and kissed her temple. "You're safe with me."

Lee felt anything but safe. The thunder and lightning might seem threatening for an instant—but Allen was the force of nature she really had to reckon with. She pulled herself free from his hold. "I can take care of cleaning up. Allen, you'd better go," she said sternly.

"You're kidding! On a night like this? The streets are wet, probably flooded, and just listen to that storm outside." The wind had picked up, driving the rain hard against the windows. "How could I possibly get back to my hotel now? I'm afraid I'm stranded."

Lee wasn't about to fall for the woeful expression on his face. "You're no such thing. Just find another cab."

"That'll be tough on a night like this."

"Well, you should have thought of that earlier." She moved to the telephone, lifting the receiver and extending it in his direction. Another bolt of lightning lit the skies outside. Lee groaned. "I hate storms."

On her last word, the electricity went off and the two of them were suddenly shrouded in total darkness. After a few indecisive seconds Lee got her bearings and groped her way to the window to look around. All she saw was the rain lashing her window. And darkness—a large segment of the city was blacked out. "Oh, no," she breathed.

As another flash lit the room, Allen joined her at the window. "Looks like I'm really stranded now. Electricity off, elevators out . . ."

Lee made no response as she contemplated her next move.

"You wouldn't be so heartless as to cast me out on a night as menacing as this. Would you?" Thunder rattled overhead, in a dramatic counterpoint to his words.

Lee sighed loudly. Cast him out was precisely what she should do, even though it would mean his walking down seven flights of stairs and more than likely spending the night in the apartment-house lobby. "All right," she reluctantly conceded. "The couch is all yours."

"Do I at least get a good-night kiss?" He reached out an arm to pull her toward him.

"I don't think so." Lee eluded his embrace. She felt her way through the darkened room into the kitchen and in a few minutes returned with a flashlight and a candle stuck in a saucer. She lit the candle and set it on the table. "I'll get some linens for you." When she returned, Allen was still standing at the window, looking down into the street. "I've got the sheets," she said. She arranged them over the couch and tossed a pillow onto the end.

"Thanks," he said. "This is very cozy. Don't you want to sit up awhile with me?"

Lee glanced around the room. Now that the storm had begun to subside, it did seem cozy, with the darkness illuminated only by the soft candlelight and the sound of rain against the windows. But it was more than cozy—it was downright seductive. "It's late," she answered abruptly. "Good night."

She went into her bedroom and closed the door. But she couldn't shut out thoughts of Allen. It would be so easy to cross that threshold; her sensations were reaching a dangerous saturation point. "I need a cold shower," she muttered to herself.

She'd better ask Allen if he needed time in the bathroom before she took over. She poked her head out the bedroom door. Allen was standing by the couch, dressed only in black briefs. "Sorry," she said, and quickly pulled the door closed. *Make that two cold showers,* she thought.

"The coast is clear," he shouted. "I'm all covered up now."

Lee cautiously opened the door. "Do you want in the bathroom before I take a shower?"

Allen lay on the couch propped up on one elbow, the sheet drawn to his waist. "No, but thanks."

"Well, good night again."

"Good night. Sweet dreams. If you get lonely, you know where to find me. I'll just be lying here wretchedly alone, wishing you were by my side." He smiled.

"I'll keep that in mind." Little could he know how true her statement was. Thoughts of him were like barnacles on her brain, seemingly impossible to dislodge.

After a quick shower by flashlight, Lee slipped back into the bedroom, carefully avoiding even a glance at the figure on the couch. She flicked off the flashlight and climbed into her bed, hoping to drop quickly into a restorative sleep. No such luck.

Two hours later she was still lying there awake, the covers pulled up to her chin as she listened to the rain batter the windows. Her mind kept wandering to the next room—to Allen, wedged between the two ends of her couch. She'd heard him get up a couple of times. He must be having a hard time sleeping, too.

She rolled onto her stomach, or tried to, but the sheet and her pink nightgown were all twisted around her from the past hour of tossing and turning. She sat up to straighten the covers and stared at the door leading to the living room. How could she purge this madness from her life? She had never felt so attracted to a man, never. Was there a cure for this disease of the mind called Allen Hilliard?

She wished Michael were in New York instead of London. If she could talk to him, maybe she could return to reality.... But with the time difference, she'd have little chance of reaching him even if she called. And what would she say, anyway? That she needed to be saved from herself? Michael would hardly understand—and it wasn't fair to use her relationship with him as a shield. Maybe that's what she'd been doing all along, under the guise of telling herself that she was simply leading with her head instead of her heart. When Michael returned, she'd talk to him, come to an agreement on the future of their relationship...on whether there *was* a future for them.

WHEN LEE AWOKE, the ceiling light was on. The power had returned during the night. She looked toward the window and saw that the rain had stopped though the sky was still overcast. The bedside clock blinked "three-thirty". That meant nothing. She lifted her wristwatch from the table. "Seven-ten." Time to get up and dress for work.

Lee approached the door to the living room, embarrassed now at the prospect of encountering Allen. She felt a bit silly at her thoughts of last night—as if he would suspect what they'd been. She opened the door to an empty room. The sheets had been removed from the couch and left neatly folded on the coffee table.

Allen must be in the kitchen. No, it was empty, too. Only a note propped up against the coffee maker. "Thanks for the couch. I'll see you tonight. Allen."

"YOU HAVE ALL THE LUCK," Maria gushed. "I can't believe Allen Hilliard—*Allen Hilliard*—just walks in and opens a bank account and then Madame Vice President gets to show him the Big Apple." Maria laughed. "I wish he'd let *me* show him the city, or better yet, a tiny little part of it—like my bedroom."

"What on earth's gotten into you?" Lee turned from pouring her cup of morning coffee. "What is the big deal about Allen Hilliard?"

"You mean other than the fact that he's a sensational hunk of man?"

"You want him? Then you're welcome to him. I consider Mr. Hilliard nothing but a pain in the neck." A slight untruth, Lee admitted to herself, but then again, he was responsible for the pain she was feeling right now. She had a miserable headache, more than likely caused by lack of sleep.

"Oh, that you could just hand him to me." Maria sighed. "I'd feel like I'd died and gone to heaven."

"Just what is so impressive about him?" Lee took a sip of coffee as she eyed her secretary. Maria, man-crazy as a matter of course, was carrying on more than she usually did about a handsome male. It was difficult for Lee to understand her preoccupation with this particular one.

"You're asking me?" Maria said. "You of all people should be in a position to know. It looked to me like the two of you were rather—"

"Rather what?" Lee interrupted.

"Nothing..." Maria trailed off. "I know you're engaged to Dr. Dayton. It's just..."

"Just what?" Lee's voice was reproachful.

"Well, engaged or not," Maria prattled on, "I realize it would be hard to resist a man like Allen. If only half his reputation is true—"

"What reputation?"

"Oh, come on, Lee. You know."

"No, I do not know. What reputation?"

"As a ladies' man. He and Charlie—"

"Charlie? Charlie who?"

Maria rolled her eyes toward the ceiling as if to suggest that Lee had taken leave of her senses. "Charlie Robin. Batman and Robin—baseball's 'dynamic duo'—you know."

"I've never heard of them."

"Surely you read the sports pages or listen to sports news every now and then."

Lee shook her head. "Not really. In fact, not at all, if I can help it." Lee had forgotten that Maria was a sports groupie who spent half her salary on season's tickets to sporting events. She, personally, had never been keen on athletics, even before her marriage to Carl Adams. And after the divorce, she had studiously avoided the subject in order to avoid Carl, too.

It would have suited her just fine never to hear his name again, and she'd rather no one ever discovered she'd been married to him. She needed to keep that part of her life forever in the past. Meanwhile she had to get her thoughts back to the present. "So you're telling me Allen Hilliard played professional baseball?"

Maria gazed at her in astonishment. "He—the two of them—were a sensation. I can't believe you haven't heard of them. After all, they were home-team guys. Charlie and Allen were the toast of New York. One or both of them was in the news all the time. Squiring actresses around town, boozing it up at bars, scuffling with reporters—the original bad boys of baseball. Then there was that incident with Charlie during the World Series—"

"Excuse me, Maria. I just remembered I have to make an important call." Lee didn't want to hear any more gossip. She couldn't care less about Charlie Starling or whatever his name was. And despite being curious about Allen in the past, today she'd learned more than she really wanted to know about him. She went into her office and shut the door, then began pacing the carpet. Her head was reeling.

"What a sap I've been," she muttered to herself. Allen wasn't just a small-town coach. He was a well-known baseball player. Which, of course, was how he'd gotten Don Stone's attention. She'd thought all along there was more to him than met the eye. She'd just never looked beyond his life in Hammond, never considered the possibility of a previous career, a previous life. There were clues; why did her usually keen instincts fail her this time? It was obvious in retrospect that Allen displayed a sophistication he had to have acquired away from Hammond. And he hadn't bought that fancy car and high-tech furniture there, either.

Allen Hilliard was a city wolf in country wolf's clothing—pretending to be something he wasn't, concealing his real identity. Of all things, a professional jock. How ironic. Not that she was an impartial observer as the ex-Mrs. Carl Adams, but in Lee's opinion, professional athletes were overpaid, overpampered, overexposed brutes, who relied on nothing more than muscle power and athletic good looks to get by. And because of the fleeting nature of sports and their short-lived time in the spotlight, most of them seemed to invest only in short-term relationships. Her experience with Carl had taught her that lesson well.

Lee reversed her stride and began pacing the floor in the other direction. Well, maybe this was good news. She'd needed a bucket of cold water to awaken her, bring her to her senses. The hour had come for Allen Hilliard to get out of her life. And this new information would help her make that happen.

If only she didn't have that dinner date tonight. Mr. Stone couldn't realize what an imposition he had placed on her. If he weren't her boss, Lee would have told him so. Especially as it was now quite apparent that Allen's baseball fame was the real reason behind her boss's unusual accommodation.

She'd originally come to the presumptuous conclusion that Allen couldn't possibly make a deposit big enough to impress Old Stonewall. But now it was likely he had. If he'd been the star Maria said he was, then Allen probably had plenty of money. Clearly, Lee had known very little about the man.

Fortunately the demands of the workday took over and Lee had no more time to ruminate on Allen. She had a number of phone calls, then a meeting with a client at ten-thirty, followed by lunch with another client. It was now midafternoon. She stretched back in her chair, then decided to walk down the hall for a can of diet cola. "Did you make reservations at the One-Eyed Greek?" she asked Maria as she passed by her desk.

"Eight-thirty. Table for two. Is that what you wanted?"

"That's fine. Thanks." She continued into the hall. Why had Mr. Stone recommended such a place for her and Allen? Lee had never been there, but she'd heard about it from a number of people. The One-Eyed Greek was popular, very *in* right now, though it certainly didn't seem to be the kind of restaurant Mr. Stone and his wife would frequent. From what she'd been told, it was crowded and noisy. Mr. Stone must have based his recommendation on Allen's reputation as a party animal.

Lee suspected that if it had been left up to Allen he would have chosen a more romantic spot for this particular date. One with soft music and quiet, secluded corners. He was obviously a man on the make, and it would be difficult to score points when your date couldn't even hear your well-practiced advances.

She smiled at the thought of Allen's possible discomfort. On second thought, this spot was probably the perfect place to take him. It would provide Lee with some protection against her own ridiculous susceptibility. Obviously she hadn't been properly inoculated against his charms. Since she *had* to have dinner with him—Mr. Stone had seen to that—she would make the best of it. It wasn't the first time she'd suffered through a meal with an insufferably shallow client. But it would be the last time for this particular client.

PROMPTLY AT EIGHT, the doorbell sounded. Lee had just slipped into a red jumpsuit of polished cotton and was fastening large gold loops into her earlobes as she strolled to the door. Another contrast with Michael, she thought. Michael usually left her cooling her heels for half an hour, sometimes longer. Allen was apparently more of a clock watcher.

Lee looked through the peephole. Yes, it was Allen, wearing a bright yellow silk shirt with the first few buttons undone, but no gold chains or medallions to block the view of his hairy masculine chest. She opened the door. He also had on blue jeans, and a sports coat was thrown over his shoulder. "Ready?" he said.

She gestured Allen to the couch. "Make yourself comfortable while I find my shoes." She motioned to her stockinged feet as she headed toward the bedroom.

"No problem," he said. "After all, this couch and I are on intimate terms."

She came back into the living room. "Shall we go?"

They rode down the elevator and made their way across the lobby to the front doors, where Phil was standing. "Have a nice evening, Miss Martin. You too, Batman." He smiled broadly at the two of them as he ushered them out.

"Thanks, Phil," Lee said. She preceded Allen into a waiting taxi and gave the driver the name of the restaurant. As they drove through the evening traffic, she glanced at Allen. "Phil called you Batman," she said. "Just like Max. What do you say to that?"

"It must be an old New York expression."

"Oh? How come I never heard of it?"

"I don't know." He squeezed her hand. "So tell me about the One-Eyed Greek."

Lee looked away, fuming. She turned around to glare at him. "So Batman is an old New York expression, hmmm? As in Batman and Robin?"

"Curses, I've been found out. Now you know I'm really the Caped Crusader." Allen smiled and slipped an arm around her shoulder.

Lee slid across the seat as far from him as possible, practically welding herself against the door of the cab. "You can cut out the cute stuff. No thanks to you, I finally know your true identity, and it's not Bruce Wayne."

"So who am I?"

"You're a rat. A first-class heel. That's who you are. Maria told me all about you. Or as much as I would let her tell me."

"And you're mad."

"Mad is an understatement. I am livid. The only reason we're out tonight is because my boss insisted. For no other reason. Please keep in mind that to me you're just a client—nothing more—and I suggest you act like a client. Or you're going to find yourself eating alone in your hotel room."

Allen cocked an eyebrow. "Do you really think I'd have to eat alone?"

His smug comment stung, but Lee retaliated without missing a beat. "Of course not. I'm sure you'd have no problem at all finding a companion for dinner. My secretary, Maria, is just one of probably hundreds of women who'd love to share a meal—or anything else—with you."

"And you aren't among those hundreds?"

"Professional jocks aren't my style."

"I'd like to be your style." He caressed her cheek.

Lee pushed his hand away. "Why did you lie to me?"

"I didn't lie."

Lee rolled her eyes and sighed in disgust.

"I didn't," Allen insisted. "Maybe shaded the truth a little."

"A little? Give me a break."

"Did I use an alias? No. I never pretended to be anything other than who I said I was."

"You were deceitful. You knew I had no idea you'd been in pro ball."

"Not at first. How was I to know Delia hadn't told you all about me?"

"Don't bring my grandmother into this. You played me along, Mr. Hilliard."

"Okay." He sighed. "I admit I was a little evasive maybe, but not deceitful. And I had plenty of good reasons for not wanting my pro career to come up. For one thing, I did a lot of stunts I'm not too proud of. Dumb childish stuff. That part of my life brought me fame, sure. But it also brought me some embarrassment and a lot of regret. It was refreshing to be able to relate to a woman without her expecting me to be Mr. Baseball, some sort of superhero. With you, I could be myself—just plain Allen Hilliard."

Lee wasn't placated. "There's nothing plain about you, and you know it. So don't try to con me. I've had it up to here with phony, superficial jocks."

"Are you trying to punish me for Carl Adams? I'm not Carl, Lee. I'm nothing like him."

"I'm afraid I see a lot of similarities."

"Like what?"

"Like lying!"

"I didn't lie to you." Allen reached over and took her hand.

"Please don't touch me," she said. "I'm not in the mood for any more pretense."

The taxi pulled in front of the restaurant. "Do we have to go through with this?" She glared at him, waiting for an answer.

Allen glared back. "I put a chunk of money in your bank and Stone promised me a dinner companion." His expression softened. "Look," he said. "We're here now and we might as well make the best of it. How about a truce during dinner? Okay?"

Lee paused. What she really wanted was to get away from Allen and go home. But he was right; this was a business dinner. No use jeopardizing her standing with Donald Stone. Besides, as happened all too frequently with Allen, she didn't have the energy to argue. After tonight though, she promised herself, she'd never see Allen Hilliard again. "Okay," she reluctantly agreed. "A truce during dinner."

The restaurant was even rowdier than Lee had expected. A three-piece band consisting of guitar, drums and bouzouki was playing Greek songs, with the diners clapping in accompaniment, as Lee and Allen followed the maître d' to their table.

Lee studied the menu, looking up each time a waiter appeared with *saganaki*, announcing its arrival with a giant throat-clearing *"Opa!"* as he set the cheese appetizer aflame. Not in the mood for pyrotechnics, Lee and Allen ordered dolmas, appetizers of rice and beef wrapped in grape leaves. The dolmas were followed by salads with chunks of Greek feta cheese, then entrées of moussaka, a layered eggplant mixture, and souvlakia, charcoal-broiled chunks of beef on skewers. They sampled the traditional ouzo, but Lee didn't care for the heavy licorice taste. So instead they opted for a bottle of Boutari table wine.

During the meal a costumed vendor approached their table with a basket of flowers. Allen selected a stem of pale pink orchids. "For you."

"Thanks," Lee stammered. She wasn't used to romantic gestures like this. Oh, sure, Michael sent flowers. But always for a specific occasion—when she'd received a promotion, for her birthday or Valentine's Day. And the flowers always came from one of New York's elite florists. There were never any spontaneous gifts...like Allen's.

What am I doing? Lee asked herself. *I've got to stop these comparisons!* On the other hand, it was dangerous to become mesmerized by the atmosphere and by being with Allen. She *should* make comparisons, she decided, but more realistic ones. She needed to keep in mind that Michael had never lied to her, had never misrepresented himself. Michael had a strong sense of honor. The only kind of honor Allen probably understood was the trophy he would get if the high-school team he coached made it to the State play-offs. Honor. That was a major difference between Michael and Allen—and Michael came out the winner. The question was whether it mattered anymore.

After dinner, Lee and Allen were sipping their cups of strong, sweet coffee when they were persuaded to move to the dance floor. They joined other diners who were standing, arms on the shoulders of the participants on either side of them, in a big semicircle. The music began and they started dancing, first slowly, then at a faster pace. Lee couldn't believe she was really out here, a party to this group exhibition, but she was—and she was enjoying it, too.

Perhaps the wine had made her less inhibited. Lee liked to dance, but sedately, discreetly. Two months ago she would never have been part of a display like this. Yet with Allen, life somehow was different. *She* was different—more relaxed, more congenial, more fun. Lee couldn't help liking herself better this way. She always tried to rationalize that every event had a purpose. Maybe this was the purpose of Allen Hilliard's coming into her life: to loosen her up. Despite her initial reluctance to this whole evening, Lee had to admit she was having a good time.

She and Allen had just taken their seats again when a belly dancer appeared and began gyrating around the dance floor, hips undulating to the fast-paced music. Suddenly the dancer was behind Allen, shedding one of her sheer veils and draping it around his head.

At the dancer's urging, Allen rose from his chair and joined her in an impromptu dance, bumping and grinding around the dance floor to the laughter and applause of the diners. "Go, Batman," yelled a couple of the patrons. *"Opa!"* shouted several others.

Finally Allen sat down and quickly drained a glass of water. "Belly dancing is hard work," he said.

"Yes, but you're awfully good at it. Maybe you missed your calling. You could have chosen the Broadway stage instead of sports."

Allen laughed. "No way. Charlie Robin and I once did a guest shot on a soap opera. I was awful—took me months to recover from the embarrassment. Charlie was pretty good and he really enjoyed it. Said he was going to consider a second career." Allen chuckled again, then paused. "That's the first time I've mentioned Charlie since Delia died. We used to talk about him a lot. What a character."

"Where's Charlie now?"

Allen seemed startled by her question. He was quiet for a few moments. "Charlie died a few months before I went back to Hammond."

Lee didn't know what to say; the mood had suddenly turned somber. Allen's dark eyes were clouded with pain. "And you still miss him."

"All the time," he said solemnly, then his expression changed. "But hey, we're here to enjoy ourselves." He drained another glass of water and joined energetically in the clapping.

The crowd was beginning to thin when Lee and Allen finally left the restaurant. "That was fun," Allen said, as he stepped to the curb to hail a taxi. He glanced at his watch. "I lost track of time. Sorry to keep you up so late."

Lee reached for his wrist to check the time. Two in the morning. "Maybe I'll go into work late," she said. "After all, this was company business."

"Sure, business." Allen's voice showed his annoyance. With a screeching of brakes, a cab pulled up in front of them. "Business," he muttered again, ignoring the taxi and drawing Lee to him, placing a hard kiss on her lips.

A flashbulb from out of nowhere exploded in front of them, momentarily blinding Lee. She quickly jumped into the cab, Allen right behind her. "Damn. Now see what you've done," she said as the cab drove away from the restaurant. "That was probably a gossip-column photographer. What will Michael think if that picture ends up in the paper?"

"Maybe he'll wonder how faithful his beloved has been while he's away in London. How faithful is *he* anyway?"

"Shut up! Just shut up!" Lee shouted. "I've had enough from you, you . . ." In her anger, she couldn't think of a name to call him. He'd really messed things up for her. How was she going to explain that kiss to Michael? She might be contemplating breaking their engagement, but she still cared about Michael's feelings. He was always so circumspect, so concerned about doing the right thing. He wouldn't understand a stunt like this at all. She could only hope the photo was just one of those random shots, that the photographer hadn't really recognized Allen.

"All hollered out now?" Allen leaned against the door, smiling at her, his wicked grin making her stomach turn flip-flops again. His brief kiss had been so intense. She hadn't wanted it to end. She'd wanted more.

Allen seemed to read her thoughts. Suddenly he was sitting beside her, holding her in his arms. His lips met hers and Lee, surprising herself, offered no resistance.

She had no idea how long the kiss lasted. Allen was the one who ultimately broke away. He rested his head against the back of the seat for a few moments trying to control his breathing. Then he looked at her and smiled. "Are you sure you're ready to end this business evening?"

His cocky smile and impudent question brought Lee back to reality, and she scowled in response. When they reached her apartment, she jumped from the cab without looking at him again. "Good night and goodbye." She slammed the door.

Allen was out of the cab in a flash. "I'll see you to your door."

"No! Get out of my life! There's no room for you. And this time I mean it."

Allen offered no retort and returned to the cab. As Lee entered the building, the taxi zoomed off into the night.

CHAPTER SEVEN

SHORTLY AFTER DAWN Lee awakened. She lay in bed a few more minutes, hoping sleep would return. Her plan had been to go into work late, but since she was wide awake, she decided she might as well get up. There was plenty to do at the office. She could spend her time more effectively at work than lying in bed brooding about last night. Lee had never experienced such a wave of anger in her life. And she'd been shocked to realize that the anger was directed more at herself than at Allen.

Lee's body still felt tense with emotion. Her mind was in a terrible whirl and the thoughts threatened to consume her. Last night's fiasco had only exacerbated her confusion. She had definitely decided to talk to Michael about breaking their engagement. Why, then, was she so concerned about his reaction? Sure, she didn't want to hurt him . . . but was there more to it than that? Was this grand longing, this overwhelming infatuation for Allen, what she really wanted? In many ways, her feelings frightened her, almost as though she'd put herself at some terrible risk by caring so intensely.

Michael was the right kind of husband for her kind of life. There were no illusions between the two of them. Perhaps she didn't feel passionate about Michael, but then again—unlike Allen—Michael didn't plow recklessly through the reserve she fought to keep intact. So what if there was no great passion? Given enough time, passion only caused pain.

Michael, Allen. Allen, Michael. She couldn't seem to stop debating which man was better for her. As if there *were* a real debate. Just because Allen desired her physically, that didn't mean he wanted to marry her. Maybe he'd said, "Don't marry Michael," but he hadn't added, "Marry me instead."

And Lee was ready for marriage. For the security of a husband and children. For the home life she'd never had. All Allen Hilliard wanted was a cheap fling. Well, Lee had no intention of sacrificing the rest of her life for a fling. She poured a glass of orange juice and gulped it down, then glanced at the clock on her kitchen wall. It was already past eight. Time to finish dressing and get to work.

The telephone was ringing as she walked into the office. Maria was out this morning, so Lee leaned over the secretary's desk and answered it. "Hello."

"Ms. Martin, please. Russ Jennings from the *New York Investigator.*"

"Just a minute," Lee said, pushing the hold button. She entered her own office and sat down, then picked up the receiver. "Lee Martin."

"Ms. Martin. Russ Jennings from the *New York Investigator.*"

"Yes," Lee said.

"Would you care to give me a statement on your relationship with Allen Hilliard?"

Even though she should have expected this question when she knew it was a reporter calling, Lee almost gasped. Why had she been so foolish as to take the call? Reporters didn't telephone bank vice presidents without a special reason.

From her experiences as the wife and ex-wife of a football star, Lee had developed a strong dislike of the inquisitive press. She'd had to field a few questions when she and Carl divorced, and every now and then a reporter would rediscover the fact that they'd been married and badger her again.

She should have been more cautious with Allen last night, should have ignored Mr. Stone's suggestion and taken Allen to a more secluded place. More important, she should have behaved as if it really was a business dinner. If she'd only realized how well known he was—she should have guessed after what Maria told her.... Lee sighed deeply. It had all been such a stupid mistake on her part. A mistake that was going to have a high price tag. Apparently that photograph was already in circulation.

"Ms. Martin?"

"There's no relationship," she said, finding her tongue. "Mr. Hilliard is a client of our bank."

"Some personal service you folks provide." The reporter laughed. "Maybe I need to transfer my account."

"Goodbye, Mr. Jennings." Lee hung up the phone. No doubt about it, the picture of her and Allen was already becoming an embarrassment. She only hoped she could explain to Michael before he heard any gossip or saw anything in the papers. But then again, how could she explain? If she remembered that kiss—and she *did* remember—she couldn't very well say it was all

Allen's fault. Her cooperation was probably quite evident in the picture.

There were three calls from unfamiliar voices in the next two hours. Lee assumed they were all reporters, and she told each one that Lee Martin was out of the office. She wished Maria hadn't scheduled a dental appointment that morning. She needed her there to run interference.

A tap on the door interrupted her thoughts. "Lee, are you in?" Great, her secretary had finally arrived.

Maria entered the office carrying a cup of coffee in one hand and a newspaper in the other. She handed over the coffee and opened the newspaper to the sports section. There it was—on the front page.

Lee covered her eyes with her hands. This was even worse than she'd feared.

"I doubt anyone will recognize you. I did just because I knew you were out with Allen last night. You are the luckiest woman!"

The picture showed only Lee's back. Allen's hands were wrapped in her curly blond hair, his body pressed against hers. The headline said, "Batman's Back in Town!" and asked "Who's His Leading Lady?"

The press would be answering that before long, Lee knew. One reporter already had a lead, and several others appeared to be on to it. They only had to call the restaurant to confirm that her name was on the reservation list. Or had Allen already told them? She wouldn't be surprised. It was the kind of thing her ex-husband would have done—and unfortunately Allen seemed more and more like Carl.

"Lee." Donald Stone came barging into her office without a knock or an "excuse me." His stern, unsmiling expression revealed all too well his state of mind. "Is this any way for one of our vice presidents to behave?" He waved a copy of the newspaper in her face.

She could have screamed, and certainly her voice was an octave higher when she responded. "Mr. Stone, that kiss is not what it seems, but regardless, *you* are the one who insisted we go out. You even picked the restaurant. Did you know reporters would be there, too?"

Her boss looked a bit chagrined. "No, I didn't, and I guess you didn't either. I'm sorry if I seem to be overreacting. But this isn't the best kind of publicity for the bank."

"I'm not exactly thrilled about it myself," Lee said. "I don't think Michael will be too happy, either."

"Oh, that's right. I forgot about him." Now her boss's face took on the gray tinge of worry. Michael and his associates were big depositors. "When does Dr. Dayton return?"

"About noon," Lee answered. "In time for the afternoon papers."

Maria had left the office. Crept out like a sneak thief, Lee thought, the minute Mr. Stone arrived. Now she stuck her head back in the door. "Lee, the telephone. I think it may be a reporter."

"Make some excuse. Say I'm in a meeting. I don't want to talk to anyone." She looked at Mr. Stone. "See the trouble I'm in?" She'd never taken such a tone or shot such a glare at her boss before. *I'll probably get fired,* she thought, and surprisingly the idea wasn't unpalatable. Right now, she couldn't have cared less. "I'm going home," she told him, "before any more reporters call. I'll be back tomorrow."

Donald Stone didn't argue; he just nodded in acquiescence.

She picked up her briefcase, then laid it on the desk. Why carry the work back and forth? She certainly wouldn't be completing any of it. All she planned to do was go home, unplug the telephone, curl up on the couch, and while away the afternoon with a paperback novel. That was usually a sure cure for stress.

Once she was home, the phone rang before she'd had a chance to disconnect it.

"You okay?" Allen's voice sounded concerned.

"Not exactly. Did you expect me to be?"

"No, but neither did I expect to see our picture plastered all over the New York newspapers," he said. "I'm sorry."

"It's a little late for apologies."

"Would it help if I came over?"

"No!" she answered quickly. "It wouldn't help at all." If nothing else, she was certain about one thing— she couldn't see Allen again. Not ever. She became too vulnerable, too erratic around him. Her only protection was to keep her distance.

"Lee—"

"Goodbye, Allen." She replaced the receiver and pulled the plug. Could she depend on him to leave her alone? Or might he just show up on her doorstep the way he had at the bank? She wasn't sure how Allen would react to her hanging up, but there was no point in worrying about it. For now, she'd just follow her plan for a relaxed afternoon. She had to fortify herself for seeing Michael later on. She suspected it would take all the ammunition she could muster to deal with the righteous anger to come.

The clock read five-fifteen when she awakened. Lee was surprised she'd fallen asleep, considering everything that had happened today. She sat up, her book falling to the floor, then moved slowly to the bathroom and turned on the shower. After she freshened up a little, she'd have to call Michael. A task she didn't look forward to.

LEE BALANCED THE SACKS from the deli, one on each hip, and rang Michael's doorbell with her elbow. She'd decided it would be best just to drop in. Obviously the incident with Allen wasn't easily explained, especially over the telephone, and she might as well face the questions—and accusations—in person. She'd dressed casually but carefully in an ivory silk blouse and matching trousers. The food was a before-the-fact peace offering. Michael loved New York deli food; the smoked salmon she'd bought was his favorite. That and the bottle of Pouilly-Fuissé might help to soften his mood.

He looked rumpled when he opened the door, unusual for the always-fastidious Michael. His shirt sleeves were rolled to the elbow and his tie and collar were loosened. "Well, this is a surprise," he said.

"A pleasant one, I hope." Lee's voice was purposely cheerful. "See?" She held up the bags. "Free home-delivery service. I thought you might want to stay in, what with jet lag and all."

"Sure...jet lag—and all," he echoed, motioning her in. "Would you like a drink?" He was holding a near-empty glass.

Lee nodded. "Maybe a little something with club soda." She followed him to the bar and set down her bags. She'd begun to remove packages and plastic containers when her eye caught the evening newspaper spread out on the coffee table. "You've seen the photo."

"No doubt half of New York has seen it. I assume the man kissing you is our very own Allen from Podunk."

"What makes you think that?" Neither she nor Michael had mentioned Allen since the day following her return. She was a little surprised Michael had made such a quick connection.

"Do you know another Allen?" he asked sarcastically. "Isn't this your grandmother's illustrious boarder?"

"Yes," she admitted, trying to hold her temper and her tongue. After all, Michael did have a right to be angry. Lee abandoned the groceries and walked across the room, past the littered coffee table, to the couch.

Michael made each of them a drink, then turned to face her. "And you had no idea he was a celebrity?"

"None." Her voice was indignant. "You, of all people, should know I'm no sports fan. I never connected a small-town jock with the professional-sports scene. How could I?"

Michael handed her the drink and sat on the couch beside her. "Do you realize this little escapade made the front page, the sports section and the gossip column? I think the gossip column is my favorite part."

He picked up the newspaper and read aloud: "'Hilliard walked off the team immediately following the final game of the series, disappearing after his game-winning grand slam. New York City hasn't seen him since—until last night. Is Batman returning to the baseball scene, or is Leanna Martin his reason for being in New York? Ms. Martin's fiancé, neurosurgeon Michael Dayton, could not be reached for comment. Is the engagement still on, Dr. Dayton?' ''

He looked at her impassively. ''Well, is it?''

''Michael, I never planned for this to happen.'' Lee's brain was spinning. She might have known she'd be identified by name sooner or later. She was used to being in the paper occasionally—she and Michael attended some important social events—but not like this. Not this tasteless display.

''So what's the answer to my question? I won't be embarrassed like this, Lee. This behavior is unconscionable. You haven't been acting rationally since that fling in Arkansas.''

''Fling? Attending my grandmother's funeral was a fling?''

''A funeral takes a few hours of your time. Not the five days you spent down there.''

''Do you want your ring back, Michael?'' She slipped it off her finger and offered it to him. As he stared at the ring, Lee felt a stab of regret. Reason had told her Michael was the right man for her; she hadn't accepted his proposal lightly, but had given it a lot of thought. They were compatible, their values and goals were the same, and most of the time she genuinely liked him. She'd neither wanted nor expected anything stronger than that. Was she doubting their relationship now because Allen had confused her?

Michael lifted his eyes from the ring to her face. ''No, I don't want the ring. But at this point I really don't know what I want. Or what *you* want. Maybe we should both take some time to think this through calmly and rationally." He stood up abruptly and walked to the bar. "How about a bite to eat?" he asked with forced casualness. He finished removing the food and wine from the sacks.

Lee returned the diamond to her finger, not knowing what else to do with it. "I'm not very hungry. You?"

He shook his head. "Not really. Later maybe. But thanks, anyway, for bringing this food over." He returned to the couch, where he stood in front of her, hands clenched at his sides. "Do you still plan on coming to the gala with me tomorrow? The hospital board expects you to be there."

Lee glanced up at him, surprised. "Of course. Nothing's changed about that. Why would you think it had? Have I ever let you down on anything connected with the hospital? I've even served on the ball committee, as you well know."

Michael ran his fingers through his hair in obvious frustration. "I'm having a very difficult time knowing anything tonight." He picked up the newspaper again and studied the picture of Lee and Allen. "You don't exactly appear to be struggling to get away."

Lee averted her eyes. What could she say?

"But then Hilliard's very experienced. He and Robin squired around half the women in New York. There were new women every week." Michael reached for his glass, then walked restlessly back to the bar and refilled it—straight bourbon again. This wasn't like Michael, drinking so much. It was evidence of deep-seated anger.

"Hilliard—Batman, the sportscasters dubbed him," Michael continued. "And he was good."

Lee's thoughts flickered back to Allen's telling her he was good—very good—but he hadn't been talking about baseball.

"The man hit in every game he ever played in. He was Mr. Dependable. But his antics off the field drove the managers crazy. The others were choirboys in comparison." He looked at her quizzically. "I never thought Lee Martin would fall for a lady-killer sports figure twice!"

Lee rose from the couch and hurried over to Michael. "I haven't fallen for him!" If she said it with conviction, eventually she would convince herself it was true.

"The man has the same characteristics you despised in your ex-husband. And more."

"I said I haven't fallen for him. What more do you want from me?"

Michael came around the bar and grasped Lee by the shoulders. "I want you to prove it by setting a wedding date."

Lee was astounded. She hadn't expected that at all. "Now?" She stared up into Michael's face.

"Yes, now. We've been engaged for a year. If Hilliard really means nothing to you, like you say, then you shouldn't mind deciding when you're going to marry me."

"That sounds like a threat, Michael." Lee spoke in a low voice, freeing herself from his hold.

"Take it any way you want. But take it . . . or leave it."

Lee's first inclination was to answer, "Then I leave it." Still she knew better than to force any hasty decisions tonight. She was no longer certain she wanted to marry Michael, but she was no longer quite as sure about calling it off, either. The emotional part of her said "Forget it"; the rational part prodded her to give the subject a rest. "You're angry and upset, Michael, and I'm not at my best, either. Why don't we talk about this tomorrow, when we've both had a little time to sleep on it?"

Michael stood silently as if groping for something to say. "You might as well stay and have a bite to eat with me."

"That's not such a good idea. I'll get the doorman to call me a cab. See you tomorrow." She kissed him on the cheek and left.

LEE WAS THE FIRST ONE in the office the next morning. She briskly went about turning on the lights and opening the blinds, then started the coffee. When it had brewed, she poured a cup and sorted through the correspondence overflowing her in-basket. She shouldn't have walked out of here early yesterday. It had solved nothing and served only to increase her stress—and her work load. Now she was even further behind. But tomorrow was Saturday; maybe if she came in then she could catch up. As it was, she seemed to be taking two steps backward for every one forward.

"You're bright and early," Maria said as she walked into the office. "I brought you a present." She handed Lee an old issue of a popular weekly magazine. Allen was on the cover.

Lee glanced at it, then handed the magazine back. "Why should I want this?"

"Well, since you don't keep up with sports, I thought you might like a quick, uh, career summary. This issue had a full bio on you-know-who. It came out right after Allen left the team. I'll just put it here." She laid the magazine on the corner of Lee's desk and headed for the door. Then she stopped. "But I'd like it back."

Lee sat down at her desk and tried to ignore the magazine. She even covered it with a file folder and attempted to concentrate on her work, but to no avail. She paced the office a few times, looking out at the New York skyscape. Finally she gave in to curiosity and picked up the magazine. Maria had marked a couple of places with paper clips and Lee flipped to the first one.

It was a full-page advertisement. "Oh, my gosh!" Back in Hammond, she'd thought Allen looked familiar; now she knew why. That same ad had been on dozens of billboards in New York. Allen Hilliard, reclining in bed on satin sheets, one arm propped against a pillow. He wore nothing but a pair of blue pajama bottoms; dark brown hair with a russet tint feathered his chest. A baseball cap rested on the bedside table and in his hand was a big glass of milk. "The perfect nightcap." The ad had caused a boom in milk sales and Lee could understand why. The image juxtaposed good and bad in an intriguingly sensual way.

She flipped hurriedly to the next paper clip and started reading. Everything Michael had implied last night was true: Allen Hilliard and Charlie Robin had led a wild life, partying and carousing. Night after night. It was as though their mission was to work their way through every party, every nightclub, every woman in New York.

And what they said was just as audacious as their behavior. The two men—juveniles was more like it, Lee thought—made the most outrageous comments, especially about women. The duo seemed to play a game of offensive one-upmanship. "Robin dismisses marriage rumors concerning his latest romance with pop singer Anita Marlow with the quip: 'I think it was comic Ed Wynn who said, "A bachelor is a man who never makes the same mistake once."'"

"Unlike his teammate, Hilliard has never been romantically linked with just one woman. Recently he's dated soap-opera heroine Tara Downing and socialite Dede Wynnewood. Gossips wonder whether the Batman spends his days with Tara and his evenings with Dede, or the other way around. When asked whether either liaison indicated love and marriage, Hilliard quoted H. L. Mencken: 'Love is the delusion that one woman differs from another.' Question: When does this guy find time to read Mencken?"

Lee was livid. The chauvinistic quotes, the juvenile stunts, the irresponsible attitudes infuriated her. Nothing was sacred, no act too risqué, no statement too daring. The two not only worked at a game, to them *life* was a game. Until the day Charlie Robin lost.

According to the article, Charlie was celebrating his team's third series win in a row with a combination of champagne and drugs. He passed out at a party and lapsed into a coma on the way to the hospital. The next day he was dead.

Had Allen used drugs, too? The magazine didn't indicate one way or the other. But it was certainly possible, Lee conceded. The thought tore at her heart.

The article went on to relate what Michael had told her the night before. Allen, with a bases-loaded home run, was responsible for New York's winning the game and series. Then he disappeared from sight.

Apparently he resurfaced in Hammond only after public interest in him had waned. Lee recalled what the grocer in Hammond had told her: that Allen said he'd come "straight from hell." Obviously, he hadn't been exaggerating. Lee told herself she should breathe a sigh of relief that he was finally out of her life. She didn't need to link up with an escapee from reason and responsibility.

But Allen apparently hadn't realized he'd been relegated to her past. Her intercom buzzed. "It's that gorgeous man on the line," Maria told her.

Lee looked at the ceiling as though searching for divine assistance. Hesitantly, she picked up the receiver. "Hello."

"Well, at least you're taking calls at the office. Since I let your home phone ring six hundred and twelve times last night, I assumed you'd unplugged it."

"Maybe I was just out. With the man I'm going to marry."

"I wish we could get that misconception cleared up. You know you can't marry the guy, Lee."

"Oh, no? I'm afraid you're quite mistaken—I can do anything I want." She paused. "By the way, I've just been reading about you."

"Yeah? Where?"

"Apparently anywhere I choose to look. Newspapers, magazines... Now I know all those deep, dark secrets you were holding on to."

"Not *all*." His voice sounded angry. "And don't believe everything you read. That reporter in today's paper has more than a few of his facts skewed. For one thing, I resent their insinuations about me. I've never used drugs, never touched them. And Charlie was not into any illegal stuff. He did hit some drugs too heavy—but they were prescribed painkillers. He'd had a lot of injuries. And he did too much celebrating with the booze. But that's it."

"Does it matter now?"

"Maybe not to anyone else. But he was my best friend and I don't like seeing him remembered like this. Why don't the papers talk about what a hell of a ball player he was instead of this two-bit gossip?"

"I haven't read today's newspaper," Lee admitted. "Maria brought me an old issue of *Personalities*."

"Oh, that."

"That. No wonder you had such fun playing me along. Not only were you a celebrity, but you were in magazine ads and on billboards throughout the country, yet I didn't even make the connection. The glass of milk must have thrown me off."

"Would you feel better if I told you my ego is crushed that you didn't recognize me?"

"Your ego could survive a nuclear attack. You probably just thought me horribly unobservant. I'm sure you had quite a chuckle over my naïveté."

"On the contrary, I thought you were refreshing. You related to me for *me*. It gets tiresome when every guy you meet wants to be your friend because of your batting average—and every woman wants to know how you score between the sheets.''

"From this magazine article, it appears you did a lot of scoring.''

"The magazine exaggerates.''

"Oh, really? You didn't say, and I quote, 'So Babe Ruth struck out some thirteen hundred times, but he also scored 714 home runs'?''

"It's not as bad as it sounds. I was actually talking baseball then.''

"And were you talking baseball when you said, 'I prefer the me-Tarzan-you-Jane approach with women'?''

"Are you going to go through the whole damn article?''

"No, I think I've made my point.''

"I've changed, Lee. I've told you I'm not proud of those escapades. I was little more than a kid when I started. A kid with too much money who looked at the world as a toy store. But that was another life. I'm not the same guy now. You know I've changed.''

"No, I don't know that. In fact, I don't know you at all, Allen. And I don't intend to. You were a brief interlude in my life, that's all. And now it's over.''

"It isn't over till—''

"Please. Spare me any more of your flippant quotes,'' Lee snapped. "This article has given me enough for a lifetime. Believe me, Allen, it's over. You will never see me, touch me, or *kiss* me again. Good-bye.'' She slammed down the receiver. "Darn. Why did I have to go and say that? Now he'll know how upset he's made me.'' She pushed her intercom button. "Maria, no more calls, unless you're sure it's bank business—or if Dr. Dayton phones. I've got too much work for anything else today."

CHAPTER EIGHT

LEE REACHED INTO THE CABINET for a glass. She needed a drink of water to cool down. The air in her apartment seemed stifling this evening. Maybe it was the warm weather; maybe it was nerves. Whatever the reason, she felt overheated, as if steam might rise from her pores at any second.

Lee considered herself a levelheaded person, in control of her life—a modern professional woman happily living in the immediate present, never giving in to old encumbrances. Now she realized that her devotion to her career and the rejection of things past had in reality been a denial, a socially acceptable and financially profitable way of avoiding hidden hurts.

Her fingers went to the diamond earrings dangling from her ears. They and the Wedgwood china visible on the kitchen shelf gave her a new and unexpected sense of having roots, of belonging. The china came from Delia—Delia Elizabeth—and the earrings had belonged to Grandmother Leanna. Lee was beginning to appreciate the value of these possessions, not for their material worth, but as legacies from her family, from other generations.

Sipping the water, she returned to her bedroom to finish dressing. Her new ball gown lay across her bed, the silky black a dramatic contrast to the busy blue-sprigged print of the comforter.

Lee slipped the garment over her head. She wanted to look good tonight. Maybe it would appease Michael, or at least appease her conscience, if she looked especially nice just for him.

Nice hardly described the dress, she decided, looking in the mirror as she pulled the zipper up just past her waist and fastened the choker collar around her neck. The gown was daringly simple—a halter bodice exposing bare arms and shoulders, a wide belt emphasizing her small waist, the full taffeta skirt flowing to a floor-length hem. From the front, her upper body was encased in the form-fitting bodice. From the back... Lee did a half turn. The back was nonexistent from collar to waist.

When Lee purchased the designer creation, she'd intended to wear it with the matching jacket. Now she changed her mind. She knew it might be considered a bit revealing by some of Michael's sedate medical cronies and their wives, but Lee felt that Michael would like it, that he would be pleased with the way she looked.

The doorbell rang promptly at eight. Lee's heart missed a beat. Michael was never on time. *Please,* she prayed silently, *please don't let Allen show up here tonight.* Her prayer was answered. Lee's caller was Michael, not Allen.

"I know you don't care to wear flowers, so I thought you might enjoy these at home." He handed her a bouquet of mixed blossoms wrapped in green florist paper.

"Thank you," she said, impressed by the gesture. She gave him a quick kiss and moved toward the kitchen to find a container for the flowers. This was totally out of character for her fiancé. Could he be feeling contrite about his bitter words yesterday? She hadn't talked to him since then and hadn't known what to expect tonight, so the peace offering surprised her.

Michael followed her to the kitchen and leaned against the counter, watching while she arranged the flowers in a vase. When her hands were no longer busy, he straightened and came up behind her. "You look very beautiful." His arms encircled her waist and his lips moved to the nape of her neck to place soft kisses against her skin. "I love you, Lee."

She turned in his arms to face him. She didn't know what to say. Why wasn't she able to respond in kind? Michael was a handsome man, a female-head turner whether in his white medical jacket or the custom-made tuxedo he now wore. Yet Lee's heart had never leapt and bounced over Michael as it did with Allen. Although his touch was now sensual, she felt no desire for his lips, for his body pressed against hers.

Lee was beginning to feel more than a little bit guilty. All along she'd assumed the two of them shared the same feelings—more "in like" than in love. Michael's declaration of love changed that. He'd never spoken such words before; it was always "I'm very fond of you, Lee." Maybe if he'd talked about love a little sooner, things would have been different. Now it was too late. So what was she going to do? For the moment, nothing, she decided. Tonight wasn't the time for a confrontation. But she knew she couldn't

continue the engagement much longer. It wasn't fair
to Michael. It wasn't fair to her, either.

A FULL WHITE MOON could be glimpsed above the
corridors of skyscrapers as they traveled across the city
in the June evening. The setting seemed to be giving
Michael more romantic ideas. He'd never even hinted
at wanting to neck in public before. Now here he was
with his arm around her, his hand resting on her bare
shoulder and holding her firmly against him. His other
hand held one of hers.

"Lee, I know sometimes I'm stodgy," he murmured in her ear. "Too often I get caught up in my
work and don't appreciate you the way I should—"

She stopped him. "Sssh. It's a two-way street. I've
been guilty of not appreciating you, either, Michael."
Have I ever, she thought penitently.

"Darling." His lips met hers in an ardent kiss.

"Michael, what's got into you?" She pulled away.
"If you're not careful, I'll have to redo my makeup."

"Don't redo anything. You look perfect just the way
you are. Like a goddess. My own personal goddess."

Lee was feeling increasingly uncomfortable, finding it hard to believe this was her Michael. Never had
he been so effusive; he was almost embarrassing her,
especially in view of her misgivings about their relationship and, worse, her guilt about Allen. She looked
out the window at the buildings passing by. Would
they ever arrive at the gala?

As though in answer to her question, their limousine turned into the circular drive of the hotel. She and
Michael exited from the limo and moved quickly
through the lobby to the grand ballroom where the

charity affair was already in full swing. An orchestra was playing "golden oldies," and fifteen or twenty couples were dancing. Round tables, each seating ten, were arranged in an arc around the dance floor, and more than half of them were already occupied.

"Very nice," Michael said as he surveyed the huge ice sculptures scattered throughout the room and the clusters of crystal prisms hanging from the ceiling, all part of the Russian ice-palace theme. A sleigh filled with donated gifts for a silent auction stood in one corner of the room. A full-length black sable coat— the auction's pièce de résistance—was draped over the side of the sleigh.

"Your committee did a bang-up job on the decorations. I'm very proud of you, darling." He gave her a quick hug.

"We're at number eleven," Lee said. With Michael's hand at her waist, Lee guided him through the maze of tables to one near the dance floor.

Two couples were already seated at the table—Jim and Diane Rosenthal, and Kevin and Sarah Smithfield. The men were physicians like Michael, the women society matrons. Lee knew both couples. Jim Rosenthal shared a Park Avenue practice with Michael.

"Hello, Lee," Diane said, eyeing her gown. "You look terrific tonight. I love your dress."

"Thank you, Diane. Yours is stunning, too. Hello everyone."

The men shook hands and the women shared the customary not-quite-kisses. Another couple arrived—Beth and Dan James—and greetings were exchanged again. The table was almost filled; only the two chairs on the other side of Michael were still vacant.

The talk drifted to weddings. The Smithfields' oldest daughter was to be married the following weekend and Sarah vividly described all the problems that had arisen during the preparations. "And when the best man broke his ankle yesterday, that was almost the last straw." Sarah paused. "But I don't want to carry on all night about the difficulties and discourage you two," she said to Lee and Michael. "Have you set a date yet?"

"Not exactly," Michael responded. "But I'm trying to schedule some time away before the end of the summer."

Lee tried to hide her shock. The two of them hadn't said a word about getting married so soon. On the contrary, she'd made a firm decision an hour or so ago to end the engagement, and now Michael was presumptuously announcing their wedding. Things were rapidly getting out of hand.

"Are you planning a big ceremony?" Beth James asked Lee.

"Uh, n-no," Lee stammered. "At least not at this point."

"But who knows?" Michael chuckled. "On second thought, we may just elope. Lee looks so beautiful right now, I'm tempted to run off with her tonight."

The others at the table laughed along. Lee was silent.

"Am I embarrassing you, darling?" Michael took her hand and brought it to his lips.

Lee managed a weak smile. If she could crawl under the table, she gladly would at that moment. Anything to escape Michael and all this talk of weddings. She glanced up and with relief noticed Hayley Hampton headed their way. One look at Hayley and everyone's attention would be diverted away from marriage and focused on her.

Hayley was wearing a red sequined dress—the dress form-fitting and plunging almost as low in front as Lee's dress did in the back. And Lee had worried earlier about being daring...Hayley had revised the definition of daring, she observed dryly. In addition to the ample exposure of cleavage, Hayley's gown had a side split exposing three-quarters of sleek thigh. The dress revealed almost as much skin as it covered.

Everyone at the table stopped in midconversation to ogle the approaching Hayley. The red dress was a perfect foil for her ebony hair and flawless Caribbean tan. Lee couldn't help but admire the tanned skin even as she realized that Hayley, if she didn't stay out of the sun, would be a wrinkled crone in a few years. Lee smiled, as it also occurred to her that it couldn't happen to a more deserving person.

The woman greeted everyone, then eased into the seat next to Michael. "Lucky me." She leaned toward him and placed a kiss on his lips, leaving a bright red smear on his face. "I didn't realize I'd be sitting next to the best-looking man in New York."

In a pig's eye, Lee thought. Lately, it seemed that at almost every affair they attended, Hayley not only managed to share their table, but sooner or later to end up seated beside Michael. Lee reached into her bag and pulled out a tissue. "For the lipstick," she whispered solicitously to him.

Michael smiled and shrugged. He took the tissue and wiped it across his lips, the red of Hayley's lipstick staining the white paper.

Hayley didn't irritate Lee as much as she did the other women. Their contempt was only slightly concealed beneath polite exteriors. Hayley paid entirely too much attention to other women's men. Boyfriends, fiancés, husbands—none were safe from Hayley's femme-fatale pursuit.

Hayley always flirted outrageously with Michael, more so than with other men, but Lee didn't get upset, probably because Michael seldom acted as though he even noticed the attention. Tonight, however, Hayley was difficult to ignore, with her glittering, fire-engine-red dress and nonstop flirting.

Even though Lee was more amused than bothered by Hayley's moves on Michael, she found the woman increasingly tiresome—maybe because she simply didn't like her. Hayley seemed vain and shallow, and a discredit to women in general. The woman was unbelievably brash, blatantly trying to seduce Lee's fiancé right in front of her eyes. Even now Hayley was resting a hand on Michael's knee.

Apparently, Hayley's behavior didn't make much of an impression on Michael, as he ignored her touch and instead concentrated on Lee, even going so far as to reach for her hand. For the second or third time that evening, Lee felt uncomfortable. Michael was not given to hand-holding in private, much less in public. Why was he acting so possessive tonight?

Lee was chatting with Jim Rosenthal, on her left, when she heard Hayley shrill, "Oh, here's my date now! I believe most of you know Allen Hilliard."

Lee turned so quickly she almost upset a water goblet. As her hands grasped the glass, successfully steadying it, she felt a familiar presence at her side. She looked up into his face. "Hello, Allen," she heard herself saying, her voice surprisingly calm.

"Good evening, Lee," he replied. Allen's dark eyes twinkled and the familiar grin mocked her. The man looked devastating tonight. Lee had seen him dressed casually, she'd seen him in a suit, and she'd seen him with very little on at all—but nothing had prepared her for how sensational he looked in a tux. A wave of sexual excitement pulsated through her veins.

"I don't believe you've met Dr. Dayton, have you, Allen?" Hayley said. "Allen Hilliard, Michael Dayton."

"Hilliard."

"Dayton."

The men exchanged the customary handshake, but their eyes were cold as they sized each other up.

"I've heard a lot of nice things about you," Allen said politely, a faint hint of sarcasm in his voice.

Michael nodded, but didn't reply. Then he turned to Lee, "Would you like to dance, darling?"

Lee had to restrain herself from answering, "Anything to get away from this table." She placed her evening bag beside her plate and moved to the dance floor with Michael.

Michael took her in his arms. "Why didn't you tell me he was going to be here?" he growled.

"Because I didn't know," she said defensively. "I've tried to tell you that Allen means nothing to me. I don't keep track of his comings and goings."

"His being here ruins everything." Michael stared over at the table. "I'd like to leave right now."

"Well, so would I," Lee said. "But we can't very well do that, can we?"

"No, I suppose not. We'll just have to make the best of it." They finished their dance and returned to the table.

The multi-course meal that followed was fraught with tension for Lee. She could hardly taste the roast chicken and creamed truffles. Michael sat stiffly as he ate his meal; Lee recognized the pose as his sulking expression. She waited for him to make the kind of petulant remark he usually did in these moods. And she waited for Allen to make some off-the-wall comment, to do something to embarrass her and infuriate Michael.

Allen, however, appeared to be on his best behavior. He was witty and charming, flattering the women and entertaining the men with tales from his pro-baseball days. The group at the table, excluding Michael and Lee, was captivated. They kept up a steady demand for more stories, which Allen delivered with self-effacing humor. Lee really couldn't fault his demeanor, but that in itself only served to annoy her as much as his presence.

After the orange mousse and coffee, and some cursory speech-making, the ballroom lights dimmed for more dancing. Lee would have liked to dance another number, simply to get away from the table for a few moments. She was irritated that, aside from compulsively holding her hand, Michael was ignoring her and everyone else at the table for a lengthy discussion with Dan James on brain scans. She sat staring absently at the dancers, wondering if Michael would finish in time for at least one more dance.

On the other hand, Michael's preoccupation with medicine did give her time to think, to confirm in her mind what she had to do. Lee dreaded the idea, but she knew there was no reason not to break the engagement tonight. After all, everything pointed in the direction of calling it quits, and the sooner she told Michael, the sooner they could both adjust to the change. She would talk to him when he took her home. But what got the message across to her now was her reaction to seeing Allen with another woman.

Allen and Hayley had left the table the moment the music started. Lee couldn't stop her eyes from following them. Hayley wasted no time in plastering her body against Allen's as they swayed to the music. Lee felt an almost overwhelming urge to dash onto the dance floor and forcibly pry them apart. Why was she responding this way? Jealousy had never intervened when Hayley flirted with Michael. Why now? Lee twisted her napkin in her lap. She knew why. With Michael, her head had ruled the relationship, but with Allen . . . Allen had captured her heart.

Not that she entertained any hopes for a future with Allen. Her body might respond involuntarily to him, but her mind had placed Allen Hilliard strictly off-limits. She'd learned her lesson about Allen's type of man long ago. She didn't need a refresher course.

Lee glanced at her watch—half-past ten. Michael and Dan were still engaged in shoptalk. Dan's wife,

Beth, had left the group to table-hop, and the other two women, Diane and Sarah, were engrossed in discussing their children. Jim Rosenthal and Kevin Smithfield were arguing heatedly about sports. That left Lee betwixt and between, and incredibly bored. She reached for her bag to go to the ladies' room just as Hayley and Allen were returning to the table.

"This old guy says he has to have a break." Hayley giggled as she tapped Michael on the shoulder. "So I guess it's your turn, Dr. Dayton."

Michael looked up in surprise, then cast a glance at Lee as though for permission.

"You two go ahead and dance," Lee said. "I'm just going to freshen up a bit." She wove her way through the tables, then, before entering the ladies' room, she stopped for a moment to watch Hayley and Michael. Hayley snuggled just as close to Michael as she had to Allen, maybe closer, but seeing them together only strengthened Lee's decision. If she loved Michael enough to marry him, then she should be at least a little jealous to see him wrapped in Hayley's tentacles. Yet the display before her didn't solicit intense feelings, only mild curiosity.

When she returned to the table, Hayley and Michael were still dancing. Allen stood up. "Since our dates have abandoned us, why don't you waltz with me?" He held out his hand.

She couldn't think of anything she'd rather do less than dance with Allen. It would reveal too much. Her feelings about him were too fresh, too open. And besides, everyone in the room had probably seen that ridiculous photograph. Surely they'd all be smirking if they glimpsed her in Allen's arms. Still, Lee didn't see how she could refuse without causing an even bigger scene, so she meekly joined Allen.

She placed her right hand in his and her left hand on his shoulder and they began dancing to "The Tennessee Waltz."

"I love these older songs," Allen said.

Lee didn't comment. She wasn't about to pretend she was enjoying this. She could imagine a hundred pairs of eyes focused on them right now.

"I hope I haven't embarrassed you by being here."

She raised an eyebrow. "Are you really concerned about my feelings? I doubt that."

"Sure I am." Allen looked into her face and grinned. "But you know how much I've been wanting to meet Michael."

"So you just had to come."

"You bet. I wouldn't have missed this party for the world."

"And Hayley?"

"Oh, Hayley's an old friend. We're very close."

"Yes, I noticed that. Do all your 'old friends' generally dance with you like two slices of bread stuck together with peanut butter?"

He laughed. "Did it bother you?"

"Of course not."

"Liar." He laughed again. The arm that had been resting sedately at her waist moved to her back, his fingers gently stroking and massaging the bare skin.

An exhilarating sensation rushed through Lee as tiny chill bumps broke out on her body. She didn't resist when Allen pressed her closer. Her breasts were crushed against his chest and she could feel the unsteady beat of his heart. Was Allen as affected as she by their closeness? Possibly, but then he was a healthy, red-blooded male; no doubt, he'd also missed a few heart beats dancing with Hayley.

Lee tried to ignore the signals her body was sending and concentrate instead on the music. But her mind was so muddled, she could no longer recognize what tune the orchestra was playing. One song melded into another, and she was lost to reality, caught in some sort of sensual web where no one existed for her except Allen.

She was unprepared when he loosened his hold and stepped back. She felt herself swaying...unsteady, uncoordinated, barely aware of her surroundings.

"What are you trying to do? Make a genuine spectacle of yourself?"

Michael's stern voice broke into her reverie. All of a sudden she realized she was in his arms instead of Allen's. Lee sobered quickly and stopped her dancing to glare at Michael. "Look who's talking. You didn't seem to be concerned about how you and Hayley looked out here together."

He pulled her closer and resumed the dance step. "That's different."

"Oh, really?"

"Come on, Lee. You know Hayley means nothing to me." Michael fox-trotted her over to a far corner of the dance floor. "Unfortunately I don't feel that same assurance about you and Hilliard."

Lee let out a puff of breath. "Look, we've already discussed Allen—too much if you ask me. Why don't we talk about Hayley for a change? She's crazy about you. Always has been."

"It's nice to know *somebody*'s crazy about me." Michael's voice was bitter.

"I don't want to argue on the dance floor."

"Then I suggest you start behaving yourself or—" Michael was interrupted by a tap on the shoulder. He turned sharply, looking as though he expected to see Allen. Instead it was a waiter holding a piece of paper.

"Your answering service, sir."

Michael took the piece of paper and quickly scanned the words. Then he frowned at Lee. "Damn, I've got an emergency. I need to get to the hospital right away."

"Well," Lee said, "no point in my staying without you. I'll get my purse and leave, too."

They threaded their way through the dancers back to the table. "We've got to go," Michael said, and explained about the message.

"Would you like us to see Lee home, dear?" Diane Rosenthal asked.

"No, please," Lee answered for him. "The party's just in full swing and I don't want to take you away—you'd miss the auction. But I'm rather tired myself so I think I'll just make an early night of it and grab a cab."

The couple left the grand ballroom and walked across the lobby toward the doors of the hotel. "I'm surprised your friend Hilliard didn't jump to his feet and announce *he* was taking you home."

"Michael, please don't start that again."

"Well, it's a good thing he didn't interfere because I'd probably have knocked him on his can."

Lee glanced at Michael, at his set expression. Did he mean what he'd just said? He looked as though he did.

There were no cabs waiting in the driveway, unusual for a big hotel. But with all the conventions in town this week, the cabbies were obviously being kept busy elsewhere. "You take the limousine," Lee said. "A taxi will be along shortly." It made no sense for her to go with Michael. His hospital was miles in the opposite direction from her apartment.

Michael acceded; he had little choice, since a patient was waiting. He gave instructions to the doorman and handed him a couple of bills, then kissed Lee firmly and possessively on her lips. "Sorry about this. I'll call you tomorrow," he said, climbing into the limo.

Lee stood on the sidewalk and waved a goodbye as the car disappeared into the evening. She felt a sense of disappointment that Michael's work had interrupted her plans for later on. Now that she'd decided to break the engagement, she was anxious to get it over with. But there wasn't much she could do about Michael's leaving, so she'd just have to bide her time. She and Michael would have their talk tomorrow.

A taxi finally pulled up at the circular curb, and the hotel attendant opened the door for Lee. As she slid across the seat, Allen jumped into the cab with her.

She stared at him. "What are you doing here?"

"Seeing you home."

"Get out of my cab this instant."

Allen leaned an elbow on the front seat. "Say pal, you have any objection to me riding along? I'm going to the same place as the lady."

"Hey, Batman! Gimme five!" The cabbie greeted Allen like a long-lost friend. "Where to?"

Allen rattled off Lee's address and the cab roared away.

"What about Hayley? Wasn't she your date for tonight?"

"Like I said before, Hayley's an old friend. She'll understand."

"I doubt that. Not even 'old friends' are very understanding about being abandoned by their dates."

"Hayley knew I was leaving. She was all for it."

Lee raised an eyebrow. "Oh, sure."

"The lady's never been interested in me. She was Charlie's girl for a time. I was just a buddy. Now her eye's on your Dr. Dayton—or haven't you noticed?"

Lee nodded. "I noticed. She hasn't exactly been a shrinking violet as far as Michael is concerned."

"Then why don't you step aside and give her a chance?"

Lee folded her arms across her chest. "Not that it's any of your business, but Michael happens to be my fiancé and he also happens to love *me*."

"Maybe he does," Allen said. "That's just one more reason you should give him up. You can't marry him. It wouldn't be fair to the guy. Both of you would be miserable."

"Maybe you're right, maybe not. But like I just said, it's none of your business, Mr. Hilliard. Can't you get that through your thick skull?"

"No. I can't seem to absorb that bit of information. I feel I have a vested interest here. For some foolish reason I'm convinced we'd be good together."

Lee sighed. "Oh, right. And for how long? A day, a week, a month? Until you tire of me and go looking for some other fun-loving female to play with?"

"Like I told you before, I'm not Carl Adams, Lee."

"Really? From everything I've read and seen in the past few days, Allen Hilliard and Carl Adams bear a striking resemblance to one another."

"We'll settle that later," Allen said with a scowl. "Right now, the subject is what you're going to do about Michael."

"What I do—or don't do—about Michael is my concern and has absolutely nothing to do with you. What can I do to convince you?"

"I think it's my turn to do some convincing...." He pulled Lee toward him and pressed his mouth on hers. The kiss was fiercer than any they'd shared in the past. It was as if Allen intended to persuade her physically that she belonged to him. After long moments, he eased his lips from hers, not uttering a word. Yet Lee sensed, as clearly as if he'd spoken, that he wanted more from the kiss—but then, so did she. She moved closer to him, a bold response for the usually reserved Lee, especially in a public cab. But it no longer mattered. Lee had ceased trying to be rational.

Allen answered the silent pleading in her gesture as their lips met again. This time the kiss was gentle. Allen's hands stroked her body. Lee's heartbeat accelerated like a sports car racing toward the finish line and Allen's kept pace with hers. The kiss intensified. It was as though neither could get close enough to the other. Both were gasping for breath when the cab-driver's chuckle intruded on the moment and they abruptly broke apart.

Allen laughed ruefully and pulled her back to him, whispering in her ear, "Lady, I can't help myself." Then he kissed her again, ignoring the cabdriver's continued interest.

Lee, however, had been brought back to reality. She drew away from him.

"Not here, hmmm?" he whispered. "You're right, of course, but I'm having a hard time keeping my hands off you."

Lee didn't respond. What could she say? As eager and accepting as she'd been, she couldn't very well chastise Allen for their passionate embraces. Where was all this leading? Stupid question, she answered herself. It was quite clear where this was leading. Straight to her bedroom. Allen would come up to her apartment and the next thing she knew the two of them would be entwined in her bed, all her promises to herself forgotten. Why was she allowing this to happen? She'd learned a long time ago to control her libido.

She glanced into the front seat. The cabbie was obviously still listening and Lee didn't want to talk in the presence of this all-too-interested stranger. But she had little choice. If Allen got her alone, she was lost. To have anything further to do with him could have dangerous consequences. For Lee, Allen had become a habit she couldn't afford. No, more than a habit—Allen Hilliard was an addiction. She'd decided to put one man out of her life tonight, now she needed to make it two.

Lee was surprised Allen wasn't pulling her back to him, wasn't continuing to badger her about dumping Michael. Instead he, too, seemed introspective. She was the first to speak. "Allen, I don't want you to come up to my apartment. I don't want to see you again." The taxi stopped at the curb outside her building.

"Lee—"

"Please. Don't say anything. There's no point in this. It's over, Allen."

"It's hardly begun," he answered.

"When it began is irrelevant." Lee opened the door of the cab. "It's still over. Goodbye." She walked into the building without looking back.

CHAPTER NINE

LEE RESTED HER FOREHEAD against the cool glass of her office window, staring blankly down at the street. She folded her arms tightly around herself as a shiver seized her body. The office seemed cold, the air-conditioning all too efficient this morning. But her chill was caused more by physical and mental fatigue than by the artificial climate.

Lee was preoccupied, her thoughts roving among the events of the past dozen weeks. Her memory focused on another morning spent staring out this window. That day had been gray and overcast, a contrast to the sun-dappled view before her now. So much had changed in such a short time—she'd been shaken to her very core in a matter of two or three months.

The scene with Allen in the cab last night frightened her. Until he came into her life she hadn't been aware that she was capable of such intense feeling. Why couldn't Michael have made her respond this way? She felt as though she'd reached a fork in the road—a road Allen Hilliard forced her to travel—and whichever way she went would be the wrong way. Her choices were a dull, predictable life as Mrs. Michael Dayton or a go-it-alone career-girl existence. It was a Hobson's choice; she knew that. But the decision had to be made and she'd already made it.

Now it was time to get to work. Lee moved back to her desk. Her output had declined since Grandmother's death—since meeting Allen, to be more precise. But she was an adult and she could get her life back in order with a little effort. She had to. Her work was all that was left now. She wasn't going to marry Michael and she wasn't going to see Allen again.

For the umpteenth time she'd told him so, and this time she meant it. Now if Allen would only accept her decision. He would have to, Lee vowed. After all, she had the right to decide who was allotted space in her own life. And she'd already determined there was no room for a man like Allen Hilliard.

The next step was to settle things with Michael. She would tell him tonight how she felt, and that would be that. Then she would get on with her life.

Lee was grateful Maria had called in sick today—not grateful Maria was sick, of course, just thankful she wouldn't have to listen to any more of Maria's prattle about Allen and Michael. She didn't need any conversation that interfered with her resolve.

The telephone rang and Lee answered. It was Michael. "Good morning, Michael. How did things go last night?" She listened to a lengthy account of his patient's distress and Michael's role in saving yet another life.

"Lunch?" Lee hadn't intended to set herself up for a high-noon confrontation. "How about dinner instead?" But Michael had an ethics-committee meeting that evening, so lunch it would have to be. She agreed to meet him at one o'clock at a restaurant they'd often patronized, a few blocks from her office. Lee felt guilty that her break with Michael would take place this way. But she didn't feel she could put it off any longer.

The black velvet ring box was in her handbag. She'd put it there this morning—a premonition of seeing Michael during the day instead of the evening? She would just discreetly slip it to Michael across the table. No one else need know what was going on. She reached into her bottom desk drawer and opened her purse to retrieve the box, then slipped the ring from her finger, inserted it into the padded slot and returned the box to her purse.

Lee looked at her left hand. She didn't feel the sense of bareness or loss she'd expected. Instead, she felt relief. *This is definitely the right decision,* she told herself. *Once I've talked to Michael, I can take charge of my life again.*

"ALL THIS IS BECAUSE of Hilliard, isn't it?" Michael was holding the velvet container and staring at it as if he'd never seen it before.

Lee wished he'd put it in his pocket, get it out of the way. The other diners were beginning to take notice of them. "No, this is because of me," she said. "It's because of *us*. It's all wrong, Michael. Surely you realize that."

"We've been engaged a year, Lee. Everything was fine until that transplanted playboy entered your life." He flipped the box open, snapped it shut in disgust, then stuffed it in his jacket pocket. "I thought you'd gone to a funeral in Arkansas, not an orgy!"

Michael's vehemence startled Lee. He was the type of man who never lost his cool. But it seemed as though he'd done nothing else since Allen had arrived in New York. Lee looked at him warily. "A marriage between us would be a terrible mistake."

Michael shook his head. "I don't agree. We're right for each other." He grabbed both of her hands in his own. "You just need to get over this fixation with Hilliard. I'm a patient man and willing to forgive everything—"

"Everything?" Now Lee was the angry one. "Just what do you think I need forgiving for?"

"It hasn't been *my* picture plastered all over the New York papers. *I* haven't been going around kissing other people."

"I've apologized for that—what more can I do? But that's all that happened. You sound as though the picture showed me in bed with Allen." Lee took a deep breath, trying to control her temper. She was breaking off their engagement; why end things with a scene? She'd try to bear up until the end of the meal and then she could escape the restaurant—and Michael. Men! She'd had it with them.

"Well?" Michael appeared poised for some sort of answer.

"I don't want to marry you," Lee said softly.

"And do you think *he*'s going to marry you?" Michael's voice was cold, the question deliberately cutting.

"That's beside the point. I have no intention of marrying him. I think I can survive quite well without either of you," Lee snapped, her patience wearing thin.

"Speak of the devil . . ." Michael's eyes narrowed. "Why does Allen Hilliard show up everywhere we are? Did you tell him we were lunching here?"

"Don't be ridiculous! Of course not." What *was* Allen doing here?

"Hello, there." Allen approached their table with a big smile, as though he were greeting old friends. "Glad I caught up with you two. Don Stone told me I might find you here. Thought I'd stop and say good-bye. I'm going back to Hammond tomorrow."

Good riddance, thought Lee, saying nothing.

"Pity," Michael snarled.

Allen ignored the gibe and looked at Lee. "If you ever need to get away from the hustle and bustle, remember you've got a place in Hammond. You can always relax at Delia's house."

Michael stood up. "You've got your nerve barging in here and making comments like that. What the hell went on down there, anyway?"

Allen glared. "Not a thing—unfortunately. Don't you trust your own fiancée, old pal?"

"I'm not your 'old pal'—and apparently Lee is no longer my fiancée. But then, you probably already know that."

Allen looked at Lee. "Is that right?" When she nodded, the corners of his mouth curved in a sly grin. "Oh."

Lee was astonished as she heard Michael order Allen to "Wipe that stupid smile off your face." He moved closer to Allen. "Better yet, let's step outside and I'll wipe it off for you. I owe you one, and it's time you got it."

Allen raised his palms in a conciliatory gesture. "Settle down, buddy. I don't want to fight."

But Michael was not to be soothed. His response was a left to Allen's chin, causing him to fall backward onto a nearby white-clothed table. Everything on the table went crashing to the floor, some of the glasses and dishes breaking on impact.

Michael paused, stared at the mess, then turned his attention to his fist, which he examined closely. "Damn, I think my hand's bruised, and I've got surgery tomorrow. That really does it—I'm getting out of here. Are you coming, Lee?"

Lee was agog. For the second time in the past few days, she felt like crawling under a table. Never, never, had she been part of a scene like this. A crowd had begun to converge around them and Lee heard someone suggesting that the police be called. The maître d' was desperately trying to calm the group. "Dr. Dayton is a good customer, a regular customer. I assure you this is most unusual." Lee was standing in front of the disarray as two busboys worked to clean up the mess. In her fog, she saw Michael disappear out the restaurant door.

Allen, now on his feet, took charge. "Send the bill to my business manager," he said, flipping a card in the direction of the maître d'. Then grabbing Lee's arm, he hustled her out of the restaurant and into a cab.

As the cab pulled into the heavy afternoon traffic, Lee began to awaken from her daze and reflect on the scene. It was almost worth the embarrassment, she decided, to witness Michael acting like a real person.

Maybe the catharsis had been good for him; he must be feeling quite superior to Allen right now.

She turned to look at Allen. Despite the fast-developing shiner, he didn't seem upset. In fact, he actually seemed rather pleased by this turn of events, the familiar sardonic grin back on his face.

"Why are you smiling? You were the one who ended up on the floor in there."

"If I'd hit back, you'd be furious with me. Sometimes you have to lose to win. Marry me, Lee."

Lee looked into Allen's eyes to see if he was kidding. Those words were unexpected. She'd never thought Allen was interested in anything more substantial than a brief affair—certainly not in marriage. There was no teasing in his expression, however; the man was serious. And now what? She needed time to gather her wits, to process this new information. "Does the proposal mean you're in New York permanently?"

"No way," Allen said. "New York is not for me. The offer is for Arkansas, not the Big Apple."

Suddenly Lee realized the taxi had stopped in front of her apartment building. "What's going on here? I have to get back to work."

"No, you don't. That bank can manage without you for a few hours. Just give Stone a call and tell him you're sick." Allen paid the cabbie and took her elbow to steer her toward the elevators.

Lee stopped in midstride. "But he'll know that's not true."

"Then tell him you're having a long lunch with me—he'll understand. If he doesn't, I'll take care of it." Allen ushered her up to the apartment, and when they were inside he pushed the telephone receiver into her hand and disappeared into the kitchen. A few minutes later as she was finishing her conversation with Mr. Stone, he returned with a small snifter of brandy.

"It's too early," Lee protested.

"Think of it as medicinal. After all, lunch was rather unsettling."

"That's putting it mildly," Lee said as she accepted the brandy. The combination of Michael's out-of-character outburst and Allen's unexpected proposal was staggering. She moved to the couch, easing off her tan pumps and curling her legs up under her.

Allen removed his sports jacket and tossed it over the back of an armchair, then joined her on the couch.

"I was serious back there in the taxi. I want you to be my wife. To come home with me, share Delia's house."

Delia's house...like a carrot being dangled in front of her nose. Lee was tempted. To go home, to have Allen. Home? What was she thinking? The whole idea was impossible. Her life, her career, her *home* was in New York, not Arkansas. She couldn't just relocate to a one-horse town and work for a pittance at the tiny local bank. Or worse yet, quit work and play house.

Allen seemed to read her mind. "I can't stay here, Lee. I've had it with the fast lane." He shifted his body to face her. "Remember how I said I never had a family? Well, that was true—until I met Charlie Robin and he became a brother to me. Or maybe even my twin.

"Charlie was like me. No ties, a loner. We met in college, both of us there on baseball scholarships. The only thing that got either one of us to the University of Arkansas was our ability as athletes. We certainly weren't great students. We were too busy enjoying life on campus as celebrity jocks to study, but somehow we managed to squeak through."

Lee could relate all too well to what he was saying about a sports figure being a college celebrity. She remembered the attention Carl had received at Syracuse.

"Anyway, both of us managed to graduate and were fortunately drafted by the same pro team. Charlie and I were in hog heaven." Allen shook his head. "It was all too much—too much acclaim, too much booze, too much money, too many women. And we were too young to handle it. At first it was great. We shared an expensive bachelor pad, had wild parties, did crazy things—you've already heard about a few of them. Then Charlie started changing. He drank too much. Not just occasionally but all the time, day after day, night after night. And the drugs—prescribed pain-killers, like I told you. But the dependency was for more than pain—physical pain, anyway.

"I should have been able to do something...to stop the decline." Allen rose from the couch. Hands in his pockets, he walked over to the window and stared out. "My best friend, my soul mate, got caught up in a world of alcohol and drugs and I was helpless to prevent it. I could do nothing. Nothing!"

Lee approached the window, touching his arm. He turned toward her and held her at arm's length. "Charlie didn't intend to kill himself—but that's what happened. There was a party one night, a party to end all parties. He and I went, even though we risked suspension by breaking curfew. We'd just won the first three series games, and we were headed for a clean sweep. Then that damn party..." Allen turned away from her and gazed out the window again. "After his death, I played the last game. I felt I owed it to the team—and to Charlie. Then I put it all behind me. I packed up and left New York."

The snippets of information Allen had shared with her in the past allowed Lee to piece together the rest of what happened. Allen wandered around the country for a bit, incognito, trying to escape prying reporters and bitter memories. Finally he ended up back in Hammond where Delia took him in as a boarder, listened to him and nursed his psychic wounds. She became a friend, a confidant, the mother he'd never had. She helped him grieve for what was past and see his way to the beginning of a new life. Lee again felt a stab of sadness that she'd missed really knowing her grandmother. Missed having her wounds nursed, too.

She could understand Allen's need for the respite, for the period of healing. But wasn't it time for him to return to a real life, to deal with the pain head-on? Lee had learned a lot during the past weeks about hiding from pain. Wasn't that really what Allen had done in Hammond?

"Everyone needs to run away sometimes," she said, "but isn't it time to come back now? Is Hammond really for you?"

"Hammond's precisely for me. And I wasn't running away. I was running *to*. But isn't the real question now whether Hammond's right for you?"

"No, I already know the answer to that question. Hammond is a pleasant place, but I don't want to live there. It's too quiet, too remote, and there are very few business opportunities. Before long I'd be bored out of my mind.''

"The quietness, the remoteness—that's exactly what's appealing about the place. And I can promise—'' he grinned ''—as my wife, you won't be bored.''

His words brought a flush of sensation. Lee was tempted to put his boast to the test, but there were just too many problems. She'd be the only one having to adjust—leaving her job, her friends, her life. And what about her cherished freedom from emotional entanglements? Allen was such a strong personality. On his own turf, he'd likely overpower her.

They were different in so many ways. How long would it take for her to become completely miserable in a small town, and how long would it take for her to tire of Allen? Or more accurately, for him to tire of her? Would one woman be enough for Allen? That aside, what kind of foundation was there for a long-term relationship? A marriage couldn't be built solely on sexual attraction—even the intense, almost magnetic attraction between the two of them. Disenchantment would set in once the newness wore off.

Lee shook her head. "I'm sorry. It just wouldn't work." She looked at him pleadingly. "You know it wouldn't.''

Allen seemed prepared to argue. "Lee—''

"Please go. Just go." Lee felt amazingly close to tears. *Don't touch me,* her eyes begged, *don't kiss me. If you do, I won't be able to say no.*

Allen watched her steadily for long moments, then yanked his jacket from the chair and headed silently for the door. What more was there to say?

"Goodbye," Lee whispered softly, then she let the tears fall, unchecked.

LEE WENT INTO WORK the next morning, her eyes puffy from too much crying. When Maria opened her mouth to inquire, Lee silenced her with a threatening look that said, "No comment." Lee was not about to have her private affairs bandied about in the office.

At noon, a sandwich and a carton of milk appeared on Lee's desk along with the sports section of the newspaper. There was a photograph of Allen next to the headline, "Hilliard Rejects Offer, Returns to Arkansas." Lee had to grit her teeth to keep from crying again. She threw the newspaper into the trash.

For the next few days, Maria was especially considerate, and Lee couldn't help but be touched by her concern. The two women had never had much more in common than their working relationship. Too often, Lee had secretly berated Maria for her lack of ambition and for her idolization of the opposite sex. Now Lee felt a pang of remorse and a new appreciation for Maria as a sensitive, thoughtful young woman. *Who am I to look down my nose at anyone else?* Lee thought. Maria had a right to lead her own life, and if she wanted to be man-crazy, so be it. That was her choice.

During the week Michael sent flowers twice and left several messages of apology on Lee's answering machine, but she'd steadfastly refused to accept or return any calls. Her wounds were too deep. She didn't want to talk to Michael, or reporters...or Allen. But Allen wasn't a problem because he, apparently, didn't care to talk to her, either. There had been no word from him since he'd left New York.

It was Saturday night. Lee, dressed in a flowing red gauze caftan, was settled in for an evening of television watching when her doorbell rang. She looked through the peephole. Michael. What was he doing here? She released the dead bolt and opened her door.

Michael's usual self-assurance was not in evidence as he only half met her gaze. "Since you refused to talk to me on the phone, I decided just to show up. May I come in?"

Without a word Lee stepped aside and allowed him to enter.

Michael raised his palms in a gesture of confusion. "What can I say, Lee? I'm sorry."

"Don't worry about it." Lee paused. "That's all water over the dam now. Let's just say you were provoked."

"That's true—I was. But I surprised even myself by my behavior." He laughed.

Lee laughed, too. "You weren't the only one surprised."

He reached for her hands. "Forgive me?"

"Of course," Lee said. "I'm just sorry about all the embarrassment."

"Well, I've managed to live through it. In fact—" Michael smiled sheepishly "—I've received lots of attention from the student nurses. I think I'm in danger of becoming a cult hero."

"You were never short of attention from women."

"Except from the woman I wanted."

Lee shuffled uncomfortably and removed her hands from his. "Would you like a drink?"

"Sure." He followed her to the kitchen and watched while she made a vodka martini on the rocks, with two olives. Michael's favorite drink—she didn't need to ask.

"We know each other well," he said, accepting the drink.

Lee nodded.

"Want to try again?"

"No," she said softly. "I don't like the way the decision was made, Michael, but it was the right decision. We spent too long trying to force a relationship that wasn't meant to be."

"Well, if I'm not the right man, then it must be my major-league competition from Podunk, Arkansas."

Lee shrugged. "No, he's out of my life, too."

Michael brushed an index finger gently across her cheek. "Lee, if you love the guy, don't let past hurts get in the way. Real love doesn't come along very often—maybe once in a lifetime. I never thought I'd say this, but I'd rather see you happy with Hilliard than alone with your memories."

Lee moved to Michael and hugged him tightly. "Thanks for caring about me, Michael. You're a nice man."

"*Now* you realize it." Michael smiled ruefully. "When it's over. Oh, well—" he tipped his glass in a salute "—here's to us and our separate futures."

LEE HAD NEVER IMAGINED that advice from Michael would be the catalyst for a decision about Allen. But after he'd left her apartment, she started thinking.

Really thinking. She'd been miserable since Allen had gone. Everything that had previously given her contentment—her job, her apartment, her clothes, the material perks of success, even living in New York— no longer meant anything.

What she wanted was Allen. Without him, it became abundantly clear that her life was superficial and empty. She'd tried hard to suppress those feelings, those yearnings to be with him, and filled her days and evenings with work. But ever since their first meeting, Lee had suspected there was more to her feelings for Allen than mere chemistry. Why had she been such a coward? Because of her failed marriage?

Lee could now see that Allen was nothing like Carl; all the two men had in common were good looks and sports careers. After that, the similarities faded. Carl was selfish and shallow; Allen caring and considerate. Lee had received that message about Allen from the people in Hammond. She'd even picked it up in her telephone conversations with Delia. More important, though, it had come through in the way Allen treated her. She was just too stubborn to notice.

It didn't matter what Allen had been in his youth, or even what he'd been a few years ago. *Now* was what mattered. The present Allen. Lee knew she could trust that Allen Hilliard with her future...with her very life. The question was whether she trusted her own feelings. Was she willing to risk offering him her love?

The next morning Lee went to her office and gave two weeks notice.

"You're quitting? Just like that?" Maria was standing in front of her desk, her dark eyes showing concern.

"No, not just like that. And actually, I think you're going to like my reason." Lee smiled. "Have a seat and I'll tell you all about it."

After Maria had left her office grinning, Lee sat quietly at her desk. If things didn't work out as she hoped, well, she could always get another job. But if Allen still wanted to marry her, she wouldn't have to worry about a job unless she wanted to work for the pure enjoyment of it. With her small trust fund and his investments they'd always have money. And better yet, a roof over their heads. Delia's roof. It was a lovely thought.

AS LEE TURNED her new car onto Elm Street, she immediately spotted Allen down the block. He was perched on a ladder, energetically slapping light blue paint onto the wooden siding of the house. Apparently he was giving the place a new look.

Lee suddenly felt apprehensive. Maybe she should have called first instead of just showing up on his doorstep. What if he'd changed his mind about marriage? What if there was already someone else in his life? Well, she'd come this far. Too late to back out now.

Allen was so engrossed in his work he failed to notice the car stopping in front of the house. Lee had climbed out and was halfway up the walk when he turned and saw her. In his surprise and haste to descend the ladder, he missed a rung and took two long steps down, sloshing the bucket of blue paint all over his jeans. Lee laughed as he stood before her. "I think that color becomes you."

"Did you fly all the way down here so you could cause me to make a spectacle of myself?"

"No. I'm sorry to say I didn't even think of it," Lee said, wiping tears of nervous laughter from her face. Then she became serious as she looked down at her toes and back up again. "I came to ask you something."

His brown eyes focused on her face. "So, ask."

"Can I still take you up on that proposal of marriage?" Lee blurted out.

Allen stared at her as if she were daft, then a wide grin spread across his face. "If I weren't covered in paint, I'd kiss you," he said.

"Coward. That's no excuse. What's a little paint between friends?" She threw her arms wide to accept his embrace, allowing her beige pantsuit to get smeared with the paint as he grabbed her in a fierce hug. Allen's lips met hers in a quick, hard kiss, then he swung her around in celebration as they both laughed.

At last he released her and looked carefully into her face. "But what about the bank—your job? New York?" Allen's expression showed concern, his usual cocksure grin replaced by an anxious tight-lipped frown.

Lee smiled. It was nice to know he could be vulnerable sometimes, too. "I'm considering a change of vocation—maybe temporary, maybe permanent. Wife and . . . mother. Right now the thought of a home and family with you here in Hammond sounds like a good career move. Can I still apply?"

"When you said maybe temporary, you were talking only job, not marriage, right?"

"Definitely," she answered. "I want a marriage as solid as this old house. A till-death-do-us-part kind of marriage. So, Batman, what do you say to another partner?"

"You're sure?"

"Very sure. Will you marry me, Mr. Hilliard?"

Allen pulled her into his arms again and sealed her lips with his own, the kiss answering Lee's question in full.

"You know what I think?" Allen gazed softly into her blue eyes. "I think Delia's legacy to me was more than just a house. She really left me you. To care for, to love . . . forever."

"Forever," Lee repeated, as they turned and walked up the front steps together.

HARLEQUIN
Romance

Coming Next Month

#3061 ONE MORE SECRET Katherine Arthur
Writing detective stories as Joe Rocco was Kelsey's secret life, but could she keep it secret when Bart Malone appealed for Joe's help in a real mystery? Bart seemed hard to resist—but was there more than one mystery?

#3062 DANCING SKY Bethany Campbell
When Adam MacLaren, with his chain of modern discount stores, invades Dancing Sky, no one is safe. Not Mitzi's fiancé or the rest of the retailers. And least of all Mitzi. She finds herself singled out for the greatest upheaval of all.

#3063 PASSION'S FAR SHORE Madeleine Ker
Dorothy had accepted the job as governess to Pearl, not because she wanted to go to Japan, but because the little girl really needed her. But it seemed that Pearl's father, Calum Hescott, thought differently....

#3064 NO ACCOUNTING FOR LOVE Eva Rutland
Clay Kencade is a risk-taker. He's got a knack for business and a way with women. So why has he fallen for serious, reserved Cindy Rogers, who's as cautious in her personal life as she is in business?

#3065 FROZEN ENCHANTMENT Jessica Steele
Jolene was delighted at the unexpected offer of traveling to Russia with the boss of Templeton's as his temporary secretary. But she soon discovered it was not going to be such fun, for Cheyne Templeton had already made up his mind what kind of girl Jolene was....

#3066 MASTER OF CASHEL Sara Wood
Caitlin resented Jake Ferriter for taking her beloved home, Cashelkerry, and blamed him for causing her father's death. But she could not deny the attraction she felt for this enigmatic, ruthless man. The feeling was mutual— but could she cope with his offer of an affair without commitment....

Available in June wherever paperback books are sold, or through Harlequin Reader Service:

In the U.S.
901 Fuhrmann Blvd.
P.O. Box 1397
Buffalo, N.Y. 14240-1397

In Canada
P.O. Box 603
Fort Erie, Ontario
L2A 5X3

Have You Ever Wondered If You Could Write A Harlequin Novel?

Here's great news—Harlequin is offering a series of cassette tapes to help you do just that. Written by Harlequin editors, these tapes give practical advice on how to make your characters—and your story— come alive. There's a tape for each contemporary romance series Harlequin publishes.

Mail order only

All sales final

Coming in July
From America's favorite author

JANET DAILEY

Fiesta San Antonio

Out of print since 1978!

The heavy gold band on her finger proved it was actually true. Natalie was now Mrs. Colter Langton! She had married him because her finances and physical resources for looking after her six-year-old nephew, Ricky, were rapidly running out, and she was on the point of exhaustion. He had married her because he needed a housekeeper and somebody to look after his young daughter, Missy. In return for the solution to her problems, she had a bargain to keep.

It wouldn't be easy. Colter could be so hard and unfeeling. "I don't particularly like myself," he warned her. "It's just as well you know now the kind of man I am. That way you won't expect much from our marriage."

If Natalie had secretly hoped that something would grow between them—the dream faded with his words. Was he capable of love?

Don't miss any of Harlequin's three-book collection of Janet Dailey's novels each with a Texan flavor. Look for *BETTER OR WORSE* coming in September, and if you missed *NO QUARTER ASKED*...

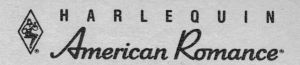

HARLEQUIN
American Romance

THE LOVES OF A CENTURY...

Join American Romance in a nostalgic look back at the Twentieth Century—at the lives and loves of American men and women from the turn-of-the-century to the dawn of the year 2000.

Journey through the decades from the dance halls of the 1900s to the discos of the seventies ... from Glenn Miller to the Beatles ... from Valentino to Newman ... from corset to miniskirt ... from beau to Significant Other.

Relive the moments ... recapture the memories.

Look now for the CENTURY OF AMERICAN ROMANCE series in Harlequin American Romance. In one of the four American Romance titles appearing each month, for the next twelve months, we'll take you back to a decade of the Twentieth Century, where you'll relive the years and rekindle the romance of days gone by.

Don't miss a day of the CENTURY OF AMERICAN ROMANCE.

A CENTURY OF
AMERICAN ROMANCE
1900's

The women...the men...the passions...
the memories....

CAR-1

Harlequin Superromance

**A June title
not to be missed....**

Superromance author Judith Duncan has created her
most powerfully emotional novel yet, a book about
love too strong to forget and hate too painful to
remember....

Risen from the ashes of her past like a phoenix,
Sydney Foster knew too well the price of wisdom,
especially that gained in the underbelly of the city.
She'd sworn she'd never go back, but in order to
embrace a future with the man she loved, she had to
return to the streets...and settle an old score.

Once in a long while, you read a book that affects you
so strongly, you're never the same again. Harlequin is
proud to present such a book, STREETS OF FIRE by
Judith Duncan (Superromance #407). Her book merits
Harlequin's AWARD OF EXCELLENCE for June 1990,
conferred each month to one specially selected title.

S407-1